GREAT BOOKS FOR GOOD MEN

JOSEPH PEARCE

Great Books for Good Men

Reflections on Literature and Manhood

IGNATIUS PRESS   SAN FRANCISCO

Cover art and design by Enrique J. Aguilar

© 2025 Ignatius Press, San Francisco
ISBN 978-1-62164-740-9 (PB)
ISBN 978-1-64229-324-1 (eBook)
Library of Congress Control Number 2024950204
Printed in the United States of America ∞

CONTENTS

Part Two

Finding Christ and Manhood in Great Literature: Reflections on Twelve Great Works of Literature

Part Four

Finding Christ and Manhood in Middle-Earth:
Twelve Reflections on the
Catholic Presence in Middle-Earth

PREFATORY ACKNOWLEDGMENT

These forty-eight reflections on manhood and literature were written originally for Exodus 90, a ninety-day
Catholic-oriented spiritual program for men. With permis-
sion, the reflections are published here in book form for the
first time. The sources for the books quoted in the following pages can be found in the footnotes. Sources are not
given for the poems and twelve great works of literature
because they are so well known that they can be found in
multiple anthologies and through basic internet searches.

Part One

Poems Every Man Should Know:
Reflections on Twelve Great Poems

What Makes a Good and Holy Priest?

From the General Prologue
of *The Canterbury Tales*
by Geoffrey Chaucer

We're going to begin this series of reflections on great poems that every man should know with some famous lines from one of the greatest poems ever written. These are the lines from the General Prologue of *The Canterbury Tales* that describe a good and holy priest.

First, however, let's say a few words about Geoffrey Chaucer, the author of *The Canterbury Tales*. He was born at the height of the Middle Ages and lived in the profoundly Catholic culture of what was rightly known as Merrie England. Such is his importance that he is known as the father of English poetry. He wrote in an antiquated form of English, known as Middle English, which is a little difficult for speakers of modern English to understand. For this reason, the spelling has been modernized in this wonderful description of a saintly parish priest.

> A good man was there of religion,
> Who was a poor Parson of a Town;
> But rich he was of holy thought and work.
> He was also a learned man, a clerk,
> That Christ's Gospel truly would preach;
> His parishioners devoutly would he teach ...

Wide was his parish, and houses far asunder,
But he neglected not, in rain or thunder,
In sickness nor in mischance to visit
The farthest in his parish, great and small,
On foot, and with staff in hand.

This noble example to his sheep he gave,
That first he wrought and afterward he taught.
Out of the gospel these words he caught;
And this figure he added also thereto,
That if gold should rust, what shall iron do?
For if a priest be foul, on whom we trust,
No wonder is a lewd man to rust;
And shame it is, if a priest take keep,
A filthy shepherd and a clean sheep.
Well ought a priest example for to give
By his cleanness how his sheep should live ...
To draw folk to heaven by fairness,
By good example, this was his business.
But were any person obstinate,
Whether he be of high or low estate,
He would reprove him sharply for it.
A better priest I believe that nowhere none is.
He waited after no pomp and reverence,
Nor made himself above reproach;
But Christ's lore, and his apostles twelve,
He taught, but first he followed it himself.

"If a priest be foul, on whom we trust, / No wonder is a lewd man to rust." How true and timely are these words. How scandalous is the sight of filthy shepherds and clean sheep. But these words are not merely true and timely. They are also true and timeless. They were written at the end of the fourteenth century, more than six hundred years ago. In the same Prologue in which Chaucer paints this portrait of a saintly priest, he also describes a worldly

Monk, whose wealth makes a mockery of his vow of poverty and whose heretical theology makes a mockery of his orthodox pretensions. As if the Monk were not cause enough for scandal, Chaucer also describes a Friar who plumbs new depths of depravity, committing acts of fornication and adultery, getting maidens pregnant, and begging from the rich so that he can keep up his life of lechery and luxury. In Chaucer's day, as in ours, there were good and holy priests, practicing what Christ preached. In his day, as in ours, there were worldly priests who put themselves first, making a mockery of the Gospel and scandalizing the faithful.

Chaucer seems to be telling us that chastity is necessary for charity. If we will not control our carnal appetites, we will be controlled by them. In order to live a life of charity, like the poor Parson, we need to lay down our lives for others. We cannot do this if we are not willing to control our passions and desires.

Immediately after Chaucer describes the poor Parson, who exemplifies the calling of a good and holy priest, he introduces us to the Parson's brother, the Ploughman, who, living in peace and perfect charity, loving God above all, is the epitome of a truly holy layman. And so it is that Chaucer shows us a couple of saints, one representing the clergy and the other the laity, who serve as candles in the dark, shining forth sanity and sanctity in the midst of the mayhem of the madness of sin.

The Last Must Be First

"Upon the Image of Death"
by Robert Southwell

One of the most challenging paradoxes with which Christ presents us is his dictum that the last shall be first and the first shall be last (Mt 20:16). What does this mean? Is Christ contradicting himself? Surely, the last can't be first, by definition, nor can the first be last? The answer to the riddle is the riddle of love itself. To love is to put ourselves last and to put the other first. The failure to love is putting ourselves first and the other last. This understanding of love also means that the Last Things must be the first things we are always remembering. The Last Things, better known as the Four Last Things, are death, judgment, heaven, and hell.

One of the most memorable meditations on the Four Last Things was written by the Jesuit martyr St. Robert Southwell in his poem "Upon the Image of Death":

> Before my face the picture hangs
>   That daily should put me in mind
> Of those cold names and bitter pangs
>   That shortly I am like to find;
> But yet, alas, full little I
>   Do think hereon that I must die.
>
> I often look upon a face
>   Most ugly, grisly, bare, and thin;

I often view the hollow place
   Where eyes and nose had sometimes been;
I see the bones across that lie,
   Yet little think that I must die.

I read the label underneath,
   That telleth me whereto I must;
I see the sentence eke that saith
   Remember, man, that thou art dust!
But yet, alas, but seldom I
   Do think indeed that I must die....

My ancestors are turned to clay,
   And many of my mates are gone;
My youngers daily drop away,
   And can I think to 'scape alone?
No, no, I know that I must die,
And yet my life amend not I.

Not Solomon for all his wit,
   Nor Samson, though he were so strong,
No king nor person ever yet
   Could 'scape but death laid him along;
Wherefore I know that I must die,
   And yet my life amend not I.

Though all the East did quake to hear
   Of Alexander's dreadful name,
And all the West did likewise fear
   To hear of Julius Caesar's fame,
Yet both by death in dust now lie;
   Who then can 'scape but he must die?

If none can 'scape death's dreadful dart,
   If rich and poor his beck obey,
If strong, if wise, if all do smart,
   Then I to 'scape shall have no way.
Oh, grant me grace, O God, that I
   My life may mend, sith I must die.

It is fitting that this meditation on man's mortality, written by a saint who laid down his life in martyrdom, should end with a prayer to God for the grace needed to amend our lives. Without the grace of God, we are doomed to a living death followed by eternal death. With his life in us, we can truly live in the very act of taking up our cross and laying down our lives for others.

As a postscript to this poetic contemplation of the Four Last Things, we might suggest that this poem be read alongside the famous graveyard scene in *Hamlet* (act 5, scene 1), in which Hamlet holds the skull of Yorick and meditates upon man's mortality. Reading this scene in the light of Southwell's poem, we will see that Shakespeare is indebted to the Jesuit's poem as the inspiration for this famous scene in the play. Shakespeare almost certainly knew St. Robert Southwell and alludes to Southwell's poetry in several of his plays. This is itself food for thought.

The Cost of Lust

Sonnet 129 by William Shakespeare

One of the wisest men who ever lived is William Shakespeare.

Although many people don't know it, and many don't want to know it, Shakespeare was seemingly a faithful Catholic living in very anti-Catholic times. In those times it was punishable by death to be a priest and punishable by death to hide a priest from the authorities. Shakespeare's Catholic perspective is evident in his plays but also in his poetry. Take, for instance, Shakespeare's Sonnet 129, which lays bare the destructive consequences of the sin of lust:

> Th' expense of spirit in a waste of shame
> Is lust in action; and till action, lust
> Is perjured, murd'rous, bloody, full of blame,
> Savage, extreme, rude, cruel, not to trust,
> Enjoyed no sooner but despisèd straight,
> Past reason hunted; and, no sooner had
> Past reason hated as a swallowed bait
> On purpose laid to make the taker mad;
> Mad in pursuit and in possession so,
> Had, having, and in quest to have, extreme;
> A bliss in proof and proved, a very woe;
> Before, a joy proposed; behind, a dream.
> All this the world well knows; yet none knows well
> To shun the heaven that leads men to this hell.

Let's look a little closer at Shakespeare's wisdom.

Lust is not merely a sin of the flesh but is the expense of spirit in a waste of shame. Even before lust is put into action physically, it has caused great harm to our souls spiritually. It lies, it cheats, it murders; it is cruel and untrustworthy. And, what is more, it is ultimately unsatisfying. It is despised as soon as it is enjoyed. In spite of this knowledge of its pernicious nature, we still hunt it. We chase it and seek it, even though we know it is a violation of our reason, a desecration of our God-given rational faculties, to do so. We abandon reason in the pursuit of the madness of erotic desire. It is a hook, baited with a seductive poison, which makes us mad once we're hooked. We are mad in pursuit of it and mad in possession of it. It promises bliss but delivers only woe, fading into a mere fantasy, a dream that can turn our lives into a nightmare.

Having been once or twice or many times bitten by this rabid beast, we do not shy away from it but continue to seek it, knowing it brings nothing but a disgusting aftertaste. We hunger for it, even though we know that it feeds rather than satisfies the very hunger it promises to assuage. It is the madness of the addict who keeps coming back for more, knowing that it is killing him.

The end of the sonnet raises the most important question. Even though we know that it is killing us, why do we not shun this fake heaven that lures us to its hell? It is because we are utterly helpless without the gift of God's help. We need his grace to heal us from the sickness of lust. Such healing will not happen overnight. It demands an ongoing relationship with the Healer. The more we find ourselves in "this hell", the more we need to call on God's help. Failure to do so will leave us happy in hell—or not so much happy as miserably resigned to our slavery. O God of infinite mercy, save us from the fires of hellish lust. Deliver us from evil.

Childlike Fatherhood

"The Toys" by Coventry Patmore

There are relatively few good poems about fatherhood.
One of the best is "The Toys" by the nineteenth-century
convert poet Coventry Patmore. It tells of a father looking
on his sleeping son, after the latter had fallen asleep in tears
following the father's chastisement of him. We will let the
poem set the scene and tell the whole story:

> My little Son, who look'd from thoughtful eyes
> And moved and spoke in quiet grown-up wise,
> Having my law the seventh time disobey'd,
> I struck him, and dismiss'd
> With hard words and unkiss'd,
> His Mother, who was patient, being dead.
> Then, fearing lest his grief should hinder sleep,
> I visited his bed,
> But found him slumbering deep,
> With darken'd eyelids, and their lashes yet
> From his late sobbing wet.
> And I, with moan,
> Kissing away his tears, left others of my own;
> For, on a table drawn beside his head,
> He had put, within his reach,
> A box of counters and a red-vein'd stone,
> A piece of glass abraded by the beach
> And six or seven shells,
> A bottle with bluebells

And two French copper coins, ranged there with
   careful art,
To comfort his sad heart.
So when that night I pray'd
To God, I wept, and said:
Ah, when at last we lie with tranced breath,
Not vexing Thee in death,
And Thou rememberest of what toys
We made our joys,
How weakly understood
Thy great commanded good,
Then, fatherly not less
Than I whom Thou hast moulded from the clay,
Thou'lt leave Thy wrath, and say,
"I will be sorry for their childishness."

Apart from being a moving and heartfelt description of
a widowed father's love for his young son, this marvel-
ous poem also serves as a meditation on childlikeness and
childishness.

Christ teaches that we must become childlike because
we will not be with him in heaven unless we become
as little children (Mt 18:3). And yet, as St. Paul tells us,
seeming to contradict Christ, when we are children we
behave as children, but when we grow up, we are meant
to put away childish things (1 Cor 13:11). Is St. Paul a
heretic, contradicting the words of Christ? Clearly not.
One who believes St. Paul is a heretic is himself heretical!
What we are dealing with here is paradox. We have to
remain childlike by ceasing to be childish. So, what's the
difference between the childlikeness that Christ tells us
that we have to attain and the childishness that St. Paul
tells us we have to abandon? The first is the wisdom of
innocence, or the sanity of sanctity, which sees the mir-
acle of life with eyes full of wonder; the second is the
self-centeredness that refuses the challenge of growing up.

The childlikeness of the child in Patmore's poem is contrasted with the careworn father who feels a sense of sorrow that the chastisement had caused his son to cry himself to sleep. He is moved by the innocence of his son's seeking solace in his simple toys to offer up a prayer for God's mercy on the childishness of man. Like the son, the father weeps, begging his own Father in heaven to forgive him and all of humanity for their childishness.

God Is Not a Tame Lion

"The Tiger" by William Blake

We all know that Christ is the Lamb of God. He is the innocent victim who is slain for our sins. We remember this in the holy liturgy when we sing or say the Agnus Dei: "Lamb of God, you take away the sins of the world, have mercy on us." But Christ is not merely the innocent Lamb; he is also King of the Universe. He is not merely the one who has mercy; he is the one who sits in judgment. His kingly status and stature are called to mind in the royal title given to him in the Book of Revelation where he is described as being the Lion of Judah (5:5), a fulfillment of the prophecy in the Book of Genesis that the Messiah would come from the tribe of Judah, symbolized by a lion (49:9). It was this latter image of Christ which inspired C.S. Lewis to make Aslan a lion in the Chronicles of Narnia. We are told that Aslan, the Christ figure in the Narnia stories, is not a tame lion.

Christ is not a tame lion. He calls us to repentance. He commands us to follow him. He insists that we must suffer as he has suffered, by taking up our cross and following him. It is this untamed and untimid image of the fearful and fearsome God, the King of the Universe and Giver of Commandments, which is evoked and invoked in "The Tiger" by William Blake:

Tiger, tiger, burning bright
In the forests of the night,
What immortal hand or eye
Could frame thy fearful symmetry?

In what distant deeps or skies
Burnt the fire of thine eyes?
On what wings dare he aspire?
What the hand dare seize the fire?

And what shoulder and what art
Could twist the sinews of thy heart?
And, when thy heart began to beat,
What dread hand and what dread feet?

What the hammer? what the chain?
In what furnace was thy brain?
What the anvil? what dread grasp
Dare its deadly terrors clasp?

When the stars threw down their spears,
And watered heaven with their tears,
Did He smile His work to see?
Did He who made the lamb make thee?

Tiger, tiger, burning bright
In the forests of the night,
What immortal hand or eye
Dare frame thy fearful symmetry?

It was surely this poem which inspired C. S. Lewis to use a ferocious and deadly tiger to be the instrument of God's judgment on the demonic forces at the end of his novel *That Hideous Strength*. The "hideous strength" of satanic scientism is represented in the novel by an ominous "scientific" organization called NICE—the National Institute of Coordinated Experiments. This "hideous strength" is ultimately overpowered by the tigerlike power of God.

Although we should be thankful for the Lamb of God, who takes away the sins of the world, we must also be mindful and thankful for the Lion of Judah, the Tiger of God, who defeats and destroys the powers of darkness. Like Aslan, Christ is not a tame lion. Let nobody dare ask him on Judgment Day, Who are you to judge?

Seeing God in Creation

"God's Grandeur"
by Gerard Manley Hopkins

Gerard Manley Hopkins, a Jesuit priest and convert to the faith who was received into the Church by St. John Henry Newman, is one of the greatest poets ever to grace the English language. His poetry is best understood in terms of what St. Thomas Aquinas calls *dilatatio*, which is the dilation or opening of the mind into the fullness of reality. According to St. Thomas, the virtue of humility gives the sense of gratitude necessary to open the eyes in wonder; it is only when the eyes are wide open and wide awake in wonder that we can achieve the contemplation necessary for the dilation of the mind into the fullness of the Real, which is nothing less than the Real Presence of God in creation.

Gerard Manley Hopkins' poetic vision is the fruit of this process of perception, which begins in virtue and ends in a vision of God's presence in his creatures. This is seen in his poem "God's Grandeur":

> The world is charged with the grandeur of God.
>   It will flame out, like shining from shook foil;
>   It gathers to a greatness, like the ooze of oil
> Crushed. Why do men then now not reck his rod?
> Generations have trod, have trod, have trod;
>   And all is seared with trade; bleared, smeared with
>   toil;

And wears man's smudge and shares man's
  smell: the soil
Is bare now, nor can foot feel, being shod.

And for all this, nature is never spent;
  There lives the dearest freshness deep down
   things;
And though the last lights off the black West
  went
   Oh, morning, at the brown brink eastward,
    springs—
Because the Holy Ghost over the bent
  World broods with warm breast and with ah!
   bright wings.

"The world is charged with the grandeur of God" because God made it. God is creative, a maker of beautiful things. He is a Poet and creation is his Poem. Since this is so, the humble heart, opening in wonder, can read the Poem and see the handiwork of the Poet in it. It flames out and shines, showing us God himself. And yet, lacking the necessary humility and gratitude, we fail to see it. We do not "reck his rod". We don't reckon on his presence. Instead, we stain the beauty of creation with the smudge of our own destructive sinfulness, treading it underfoot, searing it with trade, smearing it with our touch so that it no longer savors of divinity but smells like humanity. We have turned the beauty of creation into a human wasteland, a desert. We can no longer feel the softness of the soil and the grass because we have covered and smothered ourselves in accretions of artificiality. "Nor can foot feel, being shod." In shodding ourselves we are shedding our connection to God. We have exchanged reality for virtual reality, the real for the less real.

But all is not lost. Nature is never spent because the God of nature is never spent. He is within nature even as he is beyond it. "There lives the dearest freshness deep down things." God is the dearest freshness. It is he who lives deep down in the things he creates. His is the life in his creatures. The world is indeed charged with the grandeur of God.

God the Hunter

"The Hound of Heaven"
by Francis Thompson

We use many images to capture our understanding of God. He is the Lamb who is slain for our sins. He is the King, the Savior, the Bridegroom. For the poet Francis Thompson, he is a relentless hunter who pursues the sinner like a bloodhound. In his long poem, "The Hound of Heaven", Thompson illustrates the way that God remains hot on the heels of the sinner, even the most resolute of sinners who is trying his best to get away from God's presence:

> I fled Him, down the nights and down the days;
> I fled Him, down the arches of the years;
> I fled Him, down the labyrinthine ways
> Of my own mind; and in the mist of tears
> I hid from Him, and under running laughter.
> Up vistaed hopes I sped;
> And shot, precipitated,
> Adown Titanic glooms of chasmèd fears,
> From those strong Feet that followed, followed after.
> But with unhurrying chase,
> And unperturbèd pace,
> Deliberate speed, majestic instancy,
> They beat—and a Voice beat
> More instant than the Feet—
> "All things betray thee, who betrayest Me."

In these opening lines of "The Hound of Heaven", we sense something personal and autobiographical in the poet's voice. It is the poet himself who is the sinner doing his utmost to flee God. This is hardly surprising. Francis Thompson was raised as a Catholic and studied for the priesthood before fleeing to London to live a life of dissolute helplessness, desolate hopelessness, and destitute homelessness. Addicted to opium and befriended by prostitutes, he walked the squalid streets of post-Dickensian London, the lowliest of the low. He had deserted God, but God had not deserted him.

The poet flees from God down the arches of the years, and through the labyrinth of his own mind. He hides from him in a mist of tears and races from him with running laughter. But through it all, the Divine Hunter, the Hound of Heaven, is at his heels. The Hunter whispers to him through his tears, speaks to him in his fears, and can be heard above the laughter in the darkest dens of decadence.

The Hound of Heaven is the God who comes to call sinners, not the righteous, to repentance. He is the Shepherd, or within the present poetic context, the Sheepdog, who pursues the one black sheep that has strayed from the flock. He is the keeper of disreputable company who chooses to dine with publicans and sinners. He is the lover of the lowliest of the low who befriends prostitutes and the poorest of the poor. He is the homeless one who has nowhere to rest his weary head.

Considering that Christ in his time on earth had shared the same sort of company that the decadent poet was sharing, we might be tempted to wonder whether the Hound of Heaven was always everywhere the poet tried to flee because he was already in all those places before the poet got there. We cannot flee from Christ, however low we go, because he is already where we are. God suffers with us, even though he is not in the gutter because of his sins but because of ours. He suffers with us even though we are the cause of his suffering. When we crucify ourselves with the self-destructive nails of our own sin, we find Christ nailed to the very same cross by those very same nails. Jesus Christ crucified, have mercy on us.

Soldiers of Christ

From *Milton*: "And Did Those Feet in Ancient Time" by William Blake

One of the biggest things that we can get wrong about the Church is to believe that she is merely a human institution. Another mistake is to believe that she is purely a historical institution. The Church is not a human institution but a divine institution, founded or instituted by the Son of God. It is not purely a historical institution because she exists first and foremost in eternity. Properly understood, the Church Triumphant is the Church in heaven, and the Church Militant is the Church on earth. (The Church Suffering is that part of the Church which is on the purgatorial one-way street that leads to heaven.) Whereas the Church Militant will no longer exist when the world and history end, the Church Triumphant always exists outside of time in the eternal presence of God.

The Church Militant is the Church at war, and those in the Church Militant are *Milites Christi*, soldiers of Christ, who fight for the City of God in the midst of the City of Man. This imagery is at the heart of William Blake's mystical poem about building the heavenly Jerusalem (City of God) in the midst of the "dark satanic mills" of industrial England (City of Man):

> And did those feet in ancient time
> Walk upon England's mountains green:

And was the holy Lamb of God,
On England's pleasant pastures seen!

And did the Countenance Divine,
Shine forth upon our clouded hills?
And was Jerusalem builded here,
Among these dark Satanic Mills?

Bring me my Bow of burning gold:
Bring me my arrows of desire:
Bring me my Spear: O clouds unfold!
Bring me my Chariot of fire!

I will not cease from Mental Fight,
Nor shall my sword sleep in my hand:
Till we have built Jerusalem,
In England's green & pleasant Land.

The first verse of the poem relates to the pious legend
that St. Joseph of Arimathea had brought the Christ Child
to England. (A similar pious legend relates that St. Joseph
of Arimathea brought the chalice of the Last Supper to
England, which is the source of all the Arthurian stories
about the Holy Grail.) This wishful thinking is the inspiration for Blake's poem. Irrespective of whether the Christ
Child had walked on England's mountain's green in ancient
time, it was imperative that Englishmen should fight for the
building of the City of God in the present time.

The rest of the poem is a call to arms. The poet calls
for his heavenly weapons, and by extension he exhorts all
of us to call for ours. We are called to enlist as soldiers of
Christ in the struggle to build the heavenly Jerusalem, the
City of God, in the very midst of the satanic darkness of
the City of Man. The weapons for which the poet calls are
not merely the material tools of warfare but are mystical

weapons, similar to the miraculous sword with which
Beowulf slays the demonic mother of Grendel. The bow
of burning gold shoots arrows of heavenly desire and the
chariot of fire is heaven-bound. The sword that will not
sleep in the poet's hand is the sword of the Spirit, which
St. Paul tells us is the Word of God (Eph 6:17). These are
spiritual weapons against a spiritual foe. They are forged
in the fire of divine love to be wielded in the war against
principalities and powers. Each of us is called to wield
these weapons which have the power to defeat the devil
and his legions with the light and life of the love of God.

Being a Man

"If" by Rudyard Kipling

What is it to be a man? This is an important and highly contentious question. It is also a question that needs to be answered correctly. If it isn't, all sorts of harm can be done.

One of the most famous poems about what it takes to be a man is "If" by Rudyard Kipling. We will let the poem speak for itself, and then we will look at it in critical detail:

> If you can keep your head when all about you
>   Are losing theirs and blaming it on you,
> If you can trust yourself when all men doubt you,
>   But make allowance for their doubting too;
> If you can wait and not be tired by waiting,
>   Or being lied about, don't deal in lies,
> Or being hated, don't give way to hating,
>   And yet don't look too good, nor talk too wise:
>
> If you can dream—and not make dreams your master;
>   If you can think—and not make thoughts your aim;
> If you can meet with Triumph and Disaster
>   And treat those two impostors just the same;
> If you can bear to hear the truth you've spoken
>   Twisted by knaves to make a trap for fools,
> Or watch the things you gave your life to, broken,
>   And stoop and build 'em up with worn-out tools:
>
> If you can make one heap of all your winnings
>   And risk it on one turn of pitch-and-toss,

And lose, and start again at your beginnings
    And never breathe a word about your loss;
If you can force your heart and nerve and sinew
    To serve your turn long after they are gone,
And so hold on when there is nothing in you
    Except the Will which says to them: "Hold on!"

If you can talk with crowds and keep your virtue,
    Or walk with Kings—nor lose the common touch,
If neither foes nor loving friends can hurt you,
    If all men count with you, but none too much;
If you can fill the unforgiving minute
    With sixty seconds' worth of distance run,
Yours is the Earth and everything that's in it,
    And—which is more—you'll be a Man, my son!

There is much in these words of seeming wisdom that is very good, very true, and very beautiful. It is this goodness, truth, and beauty which explains the poem's enduring popularity more than a century after it was written. There is indeed nothing in the first half of the poem with which a Christian would quibble. Keeping our heads in a time of crisis is indeed the mark of a man, so is patience. Being lied about but not dealing in lies is the very essence of manly truthfulness; being hated but not succumbing to hatred is also highly commendable.

Having dreams but not being mastered by them seems fair enough, as does thinking without making thoughts our aim. Thought is not an end in itself, after all, but the means to an end. Triumph and disaster, the extremes of fortune, are indeed impostors. And who could argue that a real man perseveres even when his good work is undermined by the lies of others or brought low by circumstances beyond his control?

So far so good.

Now, however, things begin to go awry.

What is manly about gambling? Still more, what is manly about risking everything on a game of chance? Where's the virtue of prudence or the virtue of temperance in such recklessness? And is it really manly to be so hard-hearted or dispassionately indifferent about "loving friends" that we can't be hurt by them?

And the poem ends badly. The final lines are lies. The earth will not be ours if we follow the precepts of the poem, nor, in the final analysis, will we be a man by following the poet's advice.

A true man is one who tries as far as possible to be like the True Man himself. When Pilate says, "Ecce homo!" (Latin for "Behold the man!" [Jn 19:5, KJV]), he is showing us the perfect human being. He is crowned with thorns and is about to take up his Cross. He will lay down his life for his friends and enemies. If we can suffer scourges, if we can be crowned with thorns, if we can take up our cross to follow Christ, ours is heaven and everything that's in it. And, what is more, each of us will be a man, like the Son of God.

The Sign of the Cross

"The Sign of the Cross"
by St. John Henry Newman

"Preach the Gospel at all times," St. Francis is alleged to have said, "and, when necessary, use words."

If it is true that our actions speak louder than our words, it is essential that we try our utmost to practice what we preach. If we will not practice what we preach, it might be better were we not to preach at all. Heaven forbid that Christ could say to us what he said to the scribes and Pharisees, that we are hypocrites. Woe to us were that to be the case.

So much for those actions which others see, but what of those actions, such as prayer, which others might not see? Might it be said that we should pray unceasingly and, when necessary, use words? Isn't it true that silent prayer is best, not merely in the sense that we are not using our lips, but that we are not using words? Isn't it better that we listen to God, rather than talk to him?

Yes, it is. All the great mystics tell us so. But it's difficult for most of us.

There is, however, one surefire way that we can pray without words, and that is by making the Sign of the Cross, one of the most powerful prayers known to man. This was the view of St. John Henry Newman, who wrote a poem called "The Sign of the Cross":

Whene'er across this sinful flesh of mine
    I draw the Holy Sign,
All good thoughts stir within me, and renew
    Their slumbering strength divine;
Till there springs up a courage high and true
    To suffer and to do.

And who shall say, but hateful spirits around,
    For their brief hour unbound,
Shudder to see, and wail their overthrow?
    While on far heathen ground
Some lonely Saint hails the fresh odor, though
    Its source he cannot know.

There is no doubt at all that the Sign of the Cross is much more than a mere sign. It is a powerful prayer that calls forth the full power of the Trinity. It kindles good thoughts. It renews and awakens our slumbering strength. It gives us the courage to suffer and to act.

But that's not all. It exorcises demons. It overthrows the power of darkness. It protects us from the wickedness and snares of the devil.

But there's more. Such is the miraculous economy of grace that our own simple wordless prayer can unleash the power of God's grace in far-flung corners of the world. Others might find good thoughts kindled and slumbering strength renewed and reawakened. Others might suddenly and mysteriously find the strength they need to suffer and to do. Others might find themselves fortified against the attacks of the enemy.

Heeding the words and following the wisdom of St. John Henry Newman, we should cross ourselves whenever we see an ambulance winging its way, sirens wailing, to a person in physical need. We should cross ourselves whenever we drive past a wayside cross set up on the site of a fatal car wreck. It is astonishing to think that our own simple and silent prayer, made without words, can bring the power of the Trinity to both the living and the dead. In the name of the Father, and of the Son, and of the Holy Spirit. Amen.

Faith versus Fear

"Twelfth Night" by Hilaire Belloc

"Twelfth Night" by Hilaire Belloc is a haunting poem, full of a Yeatsian yearning betwixt faith and faerie, full of the mystical sense of the exile of life. It is a ghost story of sorts, placing it in the long tradition of supernatural tales associated with the Christmas season, and it is rooted in a particular place, specifically in Belloc's beloved Sussex in the south of England. The poet walks through the woods on a winter's night and comes upon a company of travelers who cast no shadow in the moonlight. There being no other person for miles, the poet is fearful of this ghostly company and will not walk with them.

As the poet muses on the path he had refused to take, paralyzed with fear at the haunting presence of the strange company he had spurned, he sees a star and hears the lowing of an ox. A blazing light then appears in the heart of the forest in the direction to which the ghostly company had been going. From out of the gloom, the poet hears elven voices chanting words in Latin that he had once known but which were now only half-remembered. The final stanza is full of penitential regret for the fear and infidelity, and the lack of childlike innocence, that had deprived the craven soul of the vision of the Christ Child.

Having set the scene, let's now enjoy the elven magic of this ghostly tale:

As I was lifting over Down
A winter's night to Petworth Town,
I came upon a company
Of Travellers who would talk with me.

The riding moon was small and bright,
They cast no shadows in her light:
There was no man for miles a-near.
I would not walk with them for fear.

A star in heaven by Gumber glowed,
An ox across the darkness lowed,
Whereat a burning light there stood
Right in the heart of Gumber Wood.

Across the rime their marching rang,
And in a little while they sang;
They sang a song I used to know,
Gloria In Excelsis Domino.

The frozen way those people trod
It led towards the Mother of God;
Perhaps if I had travelled with them
I might have come to Bethlehem.

This wonderful poem by one of the great Christian writers of the past century gives us much to think about. We struggle to find the right word to describe the atmosphere that it evokes. Is it sad? Melancholic? Regretful? Wistful? Creepy? And who are the mysterious travelers who cast no shadow in the moonlight? Are they ghosts? Fairies? Saints? A figment of the poet's imagination? For those who have read *The Lord of the Rings*, might the passing of these mysterious travelers remind us of elves?

These are all great questions that prove the power of enchantment the poem pours forth. At its deepest, however, it is a lament for a weak or lost faith, and a weak and lost innocence. The poet has lost the innocence and wonder that would have enabled him to accept the invitation to follow in the footsteps of the mysterious travelers into the miraculous presence of the Christ Child and his holy Mother. It might be harder for a rich man to enter the kingdom of heaven than for a camel to pass through the eye of a needle, as Jesus tells us (Mt 19:24), but it is harder still for one who lacks childlike wonder to enter the kingdom of heaven than it is for a child to walk through the door of a magical wardrobe.

The End of the Road

"The End of the Road" by Hilaire Belloc

It is said that all roads lead to Rome. This may be true on some figurative level. It cannot be said, however, that all roads lead to heaven. Some roads lead to hell. There are, however, many roads to heaven. Some take the high road of sanctity, others the low road of sin. Many of us, at one time or another, find ourselves on one or other of these paths.

The point is that each of us is on the road of life and each of us is on the journey of life. But it's not just a journey. It's a pilgrimage, an adventure, a quest for heaven. The only goal of life, its only purpose, is to get to heaven. There is no other purpose. If we fail in this quest, enabling ourselves to wander from the path, we are literally miserable losers.

The poem with which we conclude this series was published at the conclusion of Hilaire Belloc's book *The Path to Rome*, which is itself an evocation of pilgrim man, *homo viator*. In its pages we follow Belloc, as the archetypal pilgrim, whose journey toward the Eternal City of Rome is symbolic of the journey of each of us toward the Eternal City of God. In this sense the journey becomes a metaphor for life itself, indicative of the providential connection between the experience of life and its deeper meaning, the quest for Rome becoming the quest for heaven. As J. R. R. Tolkien once remarked, life is a study for eternity for those so gifted. It is in this light that Belloc's "The End of the Road" should be read:

In these boots and with this staff
Two hundred leaguers and a half
Walked I, went I, paced I, tripped I,
Marched I, held I, skelped I, slipped I,
Pushed I, panted, swung and dashed I;
Picked I, forded, swam and splashed I,
Strolled I, climbed I, crawled and scrambled,
Dropped and dipped I, ranged and rambled;
Plodded I, hobbled I, trudged and tramped I,
And in lonely spinnies camped I,
And in haunted pinewoods slept I,
Lingered, loitered, limped and crept I,
Clambered, halted, stepped and leapt I;
Slowly sauntered, roundly strode I,
And ... (Oh! Patron saints and Angels
That protect the four Evangels!
And you Prophets vel majores
Vel incerti, vel minores,
Virgines ac confessores
Chief of whose peculiar glories
Est in Aula Regis stare
Atque orare et exorare
Et clamare et conclamare
Clamantes cum clamoribus
Pro Nobis Peccatoribus.)
Let me not conceal it.... Rode I.
(For who but critics could complain
Of "riding" in a railway train?)
Across the valley and the high-land,
With all the world on either hand
Drinking when I had a mind to,
Singing when I felt inclined to;
Nor ever turned my face to home
Till I had slaked my heart at Rome.

This delightfully rambunctious poem is itself something of a pilgrimage in verse. We are invited to alter the

pace at which we read it by the poet's word choice. We are invited to slow down as the poet becomes physically exhausted, slowing in our reading of the poem as he begins to trudge, linger, loiter and limp. Particularly poignant is the parenthetical aside in the middle of the poem, which serves as a confession by the poet that he had broken his vow not to use any wheeled vehicle on his pilgrimage. Especially noteworthy is the switch from English to Latin as he switches from talking to the reader to talking to the saints and angels in prayer, a switch from the profane to the sacred that is reflected by a switch from the language of the world to the language of the Church.

The dash and dare of this wonderfully energetic romp of a poem serves as the conclusion to our series of meditations. We have seen in the reading of the twelve very different poems how great poetry can take us into ourselves and out of ourselves. We have seen how they can lead us on a voyage of discovery in which great truths are revealed and deep questions answered. We have seen how great wisdom can be revealed in a musical language and a mystical dance of words. We have seen how the beauty of poetry invites us to contemplate the deepest things that lead us to God. Such great poetry takes great time, but it is great time well spent.

Part Two

Finding Christ and Manhood
in Great Literature:
Reflections on
Twelve Great Works of Literature

Anger and the Will of God

The Iliad by Homer

Before the coming of Christ, people groped and grappled for God without the great blessing of his revelation of himself in the life, death, and Resurrection of his only begotten Son. The Jews had more knowledge than most because of their unique covenant with God, but the Gentiles were also seeking him. The greatest philosophers, such as Socrates, Plato, and Aristotle, detected the presence of God in the transcendental splendor of goodness, truth, and beauty. Their ideas were adopted and adapted by the greatest Christian philosophers, such as St. Augustine and St. Thomas Aquinas. The greatest poets, such as Homer and Virgil, also sought God in their telling of stories about the sinfulness of man and how it is punished by the heavenly powers.

At the beginning of *The Iliad*, Homer tells us that his great epic is about the anger of Achilles and its destructive consequences. He also tells us that the will of the god Zeus is accomplished in the way that Achilles is punished for his prideful anger. Other powerful moral lessons are also taught throughout the epic, each of which shows that sin leads to suffering.

Achilles' anger is caused by a dispute with Agamemnon over a woman, indicating that lust also has destructive consequences. Indeed, the war between Greece and Troy is caused by the adultery of Paris and Helen. Menelaus, Helen's husband, in alliance with his brother Agamemnon, besieges Troy, demanding the return of his wife.

Although Achilles is the mightiest warrior in the whole Greek army, Homer shows us that it takes more than physical strength and martial prowess to make a man. Morally speaking, Achilles' weakness is his pridefulness. It is his hurt pride that causes his anger, and it is his pride that prevents him from being able to reconcile his differences with Agamemnon. The moral is not merely that pride precedes a fall, though it does, but that it also causes the innocent to suffer. Achilles' refusal to fight leads to the deaths of many Greek warriors who otherwise would not have lost their lives. Ultimately, it leads to the death of Achilles' own best friend, Patroclus. Although Achilles recognizes that he is responsible for the death of his friend, his prideful anger remains. After he slays Hector, the Trojan warrior who had killed Patroclus, he refuses to hand over Hector's body to the family of the deceased for the customary religious funeral rites. Instead, he desecrates the body, dragging it around the walls of Troy in full view of Hector's family. This angers the gods, who force Achilles to return the body.

Toward the end of the epic, Homer gives examples of magnanimity and forgiveness during an athletic contest to show metaphorically that it is these virtues that restore peace, whereas their absence causes division and destruction.

The lesson that Homer teaches is clear enough. Manhood is not merely about physical strength. A great warrior is not necessarily a great man. Greatness is connected to the practice of virtue. Achilles' pride leads to anger, which leads to the desire for vengeance, and this, in turn, leads to great suffering. Nor is it only the prideful person who suffers. His friends suffer as much as his enemies. There are no winners when pride gives way to anger. There are only losers. Pride precedes a fall. The proud man is not a good man, nor is he a true man. He is a miserable loser. This is the lesson that God teaches and that we are meant to learn.

The Journey Home

The Odyssey by Homer

Great literature teaches us that there are two types of men. First, there is *homo viator*, which can be translated as "man on a journey" or "man on a quest" or, on a deeper level, "man on a pilgrimage" or "pilgrim man". This understanding of who we are means that we need to see our lives as a journey, or a quest, or a pilgrimage. The other type of man of whom literature teaches is *homo superbus*, which means "proud man" or "prideful man". The proud man does not want to go on the quest of life but wants to do his own thing and go his own way. He doesn't want to go on the appointed journey. He doesn't want to take up his cross and follow Christ; he wants to be left alone to do as he wishes.

The problem, as literature also teaches, is that each of us is both of them. Each of us is *homo viator* and *homo superbus*. We are pilgrim men, but we are also proud men. We are called to go on the pilgrimage of life, but we are tempted to refuse the sacrifices that the pilgrimage demands. This is why Russian novelist Aleksandr Solzhenitsyn proclaims that the battle between good and evil takes place in each individual heart. This is the civil war, or the very uncivil war, between *homo viator* and *homo superbus* in each of our hearts.

The archetypal *homo viator* in all of literature is Odysseus, the hero of Homer's epic *The Odyssey*. In some ways, *The Odyssey* can be seen as a sequel to *The Iliad* because the story begins after the end of the siege of Troy, which is the setting for Homer's earlier epic. It recounts the many journeys of Odysseus as he tries to get back home to his wife and son following the war. It is the archetypal "journey home" that invites metaphorical comparisons with the quest of the Christian to reach his heavenly home, this being the ultimate and only true purpose of the journey of life.

Odysseus' odyssey, his journey home, takes ten years because he is punished by the gods for his pridefulness and recklessness. Throughout the journey, he learns humility and wisdom through the experience of suffering. This is Homer's moral, as is clear from his words, placed on the lips of Zeus at the very beginning of the epic, that men blame the gods for suffering, whereas most suffering is caused by human recklessness, except for that which is "given". In this way, Homer grapples manfully with the mystery of suffering, or the problem of pain as C. S. Lewis calls it. Most suffering is the consequence of sin, but some suffering is "given" as a gift to help us grow in wisdom and virtue.

Odysseus suffers from his own recklessness, but he also accepts suffering as a gift. This is epitomized symbolically when he returns home disguised as a beggar and not in triumph as a king and war hero. He suffers abuse at the hands of the most villainous of men who are squatting as unwelcome guests in his own home. Instead of inflicting suffering on others through his sins, he has become the innocent victim of the sins of others. He has learned the priceless lesson that the journey of life had taught him. He has learned that *homo superbus* is the enemy within who must be conquered if the goal of homecoming is to be attained, and he learns that humility and wisdom are ultimately the same thing.

Prisoners of Lust

The Aeneid by Virgil

We have already seen, in our reflection on *The Iliad* of Homer, that pride and lust cause chaos, war, and suffering. It is said of Helen that she was so beautiful that her face launched a thousand ships. This was the armada that sailed from Greece to demand her return after she had deserted her husband and family to elope with Paris, the handsome prince of Troy. The ensuing siege of Troy lasted ten years and led to the destruction of the city. Such is the destructive power of lust and adultery.

This power is seen in the story of Aeneas and Dido, one of the most tragic of love stories, which is told by Virgil in his epic poem, *The Aeneid*.

Like Odysseus, Aeneas is on a journey home. There is a difference, however. Whereas Odysseus was trying to get back to his old home to be reunited with his wife and son, Aeneas is on a mission to find a new home after his old home of Troy had been destroyed by the Greeks. He is, therefore, a refugee from an old war and also a pioneer and founding father of a new world. It is Aeneas' divinely appointed mission to found the new city of Rome, the Eternal City, which is destined to conquer the world. This is the will of the god Jove. Aeneas has a divine duty to do the god's will.

All goes well until Aeneas and his men land at the city of Carthage. Aeneas falls madly in love with Dido, Carthage's beautiful queen, and she with him. Note the all too true phrase "*madly* in love". There is nothing rational or responsible in their relationship. Only having eyes for each other, they neglect their responsibilities to their own people:

> In those days Rumor took an evil joy
> At filling countrysides with whispers, whispers,
> Gossip of what was done, and never done:
> How this Aeneas landed, Trojan born,
> How Dido in her beauty graced his company,
> Then how they reveled all the winter long
> Unmindful of the realm, prisoners of lust.

In neglecting their duty and doing their own thing, they had become "prisoners of lust", slaves to their own passion, and had become "careless of their good name". Aeneas had forgotten his divine mission to find and found Rome; Dido was neglecting her own people and realm. This angers the god Jove, who sends his messenger to remind Aeneas of his god-given responsibilities. "Correct him", Jove commands. "If he will not strive for his own honour, does he begrudge his son, Ascanius, the high strongholds of Rome?" Thus, in no uncertain terms, does Jove remind Aeneas that the honor of his manhood demands that he do his duty, and, if this does not persuade him, that the duties of fatherhood demand that he sacrifice himself for the good of his son.

Coming to his senses, Aeneas resolves to leave and breaks the news to the distraught Dido. He explains that he owes it to his son, whom he had "wronged" and who would be "defrauded of his kingdom" by Aeneas' neglect of his mission. And, what is more, he knows that the founding of Rome is the will of god. "So please," he concludes, "no more of these appeals that set us both afire. I sail for Italy not of my own free will."

It is not strictly true that Aeneas is not acting of his own free will. He knows what he is doing and is choosing to do it. What he means is that he is doing what he must, as a man and as a father, and not what he wants. He is showing that true love is not about the gratification of desire but about acting responsibly for the good of others. "Unconscionable love," Virgil writes, "to what extremes will you not drive our hearts!" This is profound wisdom that harmonizes with the Christian understanding of love. If love is unconscionable, if it is divorced from a healthy conscience, it will do great harm to ourselves and others. In Dido's case, her unconscionable love drives her to despair. She commits suicide in a final act of betrayal of her people and of herself. Those who are prisoners of lust are not free, irrespective of how much they talk of freedom, nor are they rational. On the contrary, lust is an act of treason against reason.

The Weakness of the Warrior

Beowulf by Anonymous

Having focused on the great epics of ancient Greece and Rome, we'll now turn our attention to *Beowulf*, the great Anglo-Saxon epic.

Beowulf was probably written in the early eighth century by an anonymous Anglo-Saxon monk who was a contemporary of that other great Anglo-Saxon monk, St. Bede the Venerable. It tells of the life and adventures of the eponymous hero who is reputed to be the most powerful man alive and the greatest warrior of his age. The epic is divided into three parts. In each part, Beowulf fights a different demonic monster. In the first part, he fights and defeats the monstrous Grendel; in the second part, he fights and defeats Grendel's mother; and in the final part, he fights and defeats the dragon but is fatally wounded in doing so.

Grendel is described as "a powerful demon, a prowler through the dark" and "a fiend out of hell" who is angered by a poet's retelling of the story of Creation from the Book of Genesis. In vengeance, he begins to attack the people of Denmark, killing many. No Danish warrior is able to defeat him. The kingdom is, therefore, defenseless. It is then that Beowulf arrives on the scene, "the man who of all men was foremost and strongest in the days of this life". He is so powerful and such a great warrior that he announces his intention to fight the monster in unarmed combat:

I have heard ... that the monster scorns
In his reckless way to use weapons ...
    I hereby renounce
Sword and blade and the shelter of the broad shield,
The heavy war-board; hand-to-hand
Is how it will be, a life-and-death
Fight with the fiend.

Beowulf places "complete trust in his strength of limb and the Lord's favor" and prays that the will of God be done:

    And may the Divine Lord
    In His wisdom grant the glory of victory
    To whichever side He sees fit.

After Beowulf's victory over Grendel, the wrath of Grendel's mother, the "monstrous hell-bride", descends on the people. Beowulf prepares to fight this new foe, but this time he will be armed with an ancient sword that had never failed in battle. He has, therefore, not merely his own physical strength but also the best that human technology has to offer. As battle commences, Beowulf discovers that the sword is powerless against the supernatural demonic power of this new monster. He casts it aside and is forced to rely on "the might of his arm". He soon realizes that this will not suffice either. Grendel's mother is too strong for him. It is then that "the Lord, the Ruler of Heaven," sends a supernatural sword, and it is with this weapon that Beowulf strikes the fatal blow against the demonic bride from hell.

This time, Beowulf does not glory in his own strength, which had failed him, nor in the glory of human technology, the sword also having failed him. "If God had not helped me," he states, "the outcome would have been quick and fatal." To God be the glory!

The "magic" or miraculous sword, which God had provided, dissolves after it has done its job in slaying the demonic power. Only the hilt remains on which are carved scenes from salvation history. This sword, as a supernatural gift from God, symbolizes grace, without which even the mightiest warrior cannot defeat the power of evil. *Beowulf* is, therefore, a cautionary tale about the dangers of "self-help" spirituality, which was as fashionable in Anglo-Saxon times as it is fashionable today. In those days it was known as Pelagianism, taking its name from the heretical Pelagius, who taught that men could get to heaven merely through the triumph of their own strength of will. Since we achieve salvation by merely doing what Christ commanded, Pelagius claimed, there was no need for grace, or the sacraments, or the Church. People, if they were strong enough in faith, could simply save themselves. The monk who wrote *Beowulf* shows that even the mightiest of men armed with the mightiest of man-made weapons cannot defeat the power of evil without the gift of God's supernatural assistance, which theologians call grace.

Looking Sin in the Eye

The Divine Comedy by Dante

With the arguable exception of Homer's epics, which we have discussed already, Dante's *Divine Comedy* is probably the greatest work of literature ever written. Dante places himself in the story as a character, making the work a spiritual autobiography in a strange sort of way, but it is also a story with universal significance to everyone who reads it. It shows us ourselves. It holds up a mirror to humanity and, therefore, by extension, it holds up a mirror to each individual human person. In this sense, Dante in the story is an Everyman figure. He is our representative.

The story begins with Dante finding himself lost in the dark wood of sin into which he'd strayed. He cannot escape because wild beasts representing the seven deadly sins are hounding him. He is lost. Trapped. He cannot escape without divine intervention. This comes in the form of the communion of saints, whose prayers have the power to release Dante from the darkness. The principal intercessor on Dante's behalf is the Blessed Virgin. It is she who sends St. Lucy, the patron saint of the blind, to Beatrice, the woman whom Dante loves who has died tragically young. Beatrice, in turn, sends the shade of the poet Virgil to serve as Dante's guide.

Virgil explains that the only way out of the dark wood of sin is downward. They must enter through the gates of hell itself. The first part of the *Divine Comedy* recounts Dante's descent through the various levels of hell, each representing one of the deadly sins. In each of these circles of hell, he meets the souls of those who have been condemned to that particular circle because of the particular unrepented mortal sins that they had committed in life. This allows Dante, and us, to understand better the destructive ugliness of sin and its eternal and infernal consequences.

Having looked each of the deadly sins in the eye, seeing them with doom-laden clarity, he is now ready to make the ascent of Mount Purgatory. This ascent is possible only with the assent of the penitential soul. It is, therefore, with a spirit of true repentance, inspired by his deeper knowledge of the deadliness of sin, that Dante begins to climb purgatorially. As he ascends higher and higher, he passes through various levels of the mountain on which sinners are being purged of the sins they've committed. As with hell, each of the seven deadly sins has its assigned place on the mountain. Once again, Dante comes face-to-face with sinners, but this time he sees those who embrace their purgatorial suffering joyfully as the means of cleansing them from their sinfulness and enabling them to ascend into the presence of God.

Having climbed the mountain, Dante then ascends from its summit into heaven itself, where he meets many individual saints. St. Thomas Aquinas is revealed as the spokesman of the wise and as Dante's mentor, a reflection of the author's own reverence for the Angelic Doctor. St. Peter examines Dante in the virtue of faith; St. James examines him in the virtue of hope; and St. John examines him in the virtue of love. It is here that Dante's love for Beatrice is consummated through its purification. He now sees her with the clarity of charity, which has purified his love, removing the remnant of the stains of eros that had sullied and soiled his love for her in the past. His vision purified, he now beholds Purity Herself, the Blessed Virgin Mary. It is through her intercession that Dante is moved to the ecstasy of the Beatific Vision, seeing the Triune Incarnate God.

The mystical backdrop of the soul's ascent to God through its assent to God's will is reflected in the fact that Dante descends into hell on Holy Thursday and emerges into the light at the foot of Mount Purgatory at dawn on Easter Sunday. He is, therefore, mystically united to the suffering, death, and Resurrection of Christ in his own journey from the dark wood of sin to the presence of God in paradise. His journey is ours. His assent is the assent that we need to give. His ascent, aided by the intercession of the saints, is the way to heaven.

"To Be or Not to Be"

Hamlet by William Shakespeare

Hamlet is one of the most famous men in the history of literature. The words he speaks at the beginning of his famous soliloquy, "To be or not to be", are some of the most famous lines in all of literature. What is not as well known is the way in which Hamlet teaches priceless lessons about manhood and about man's relationship with God.

As with Dante in *The Divine Comedy*, the eponymous hero of Shakespeare's play begins in a dark place of sin but ends by uniting himself to the will of God and by laying down his life for his friends and country. As such, his is a journey we would do well to contemplate and emulate.

The play begins with Hamlet's mourning the recent death of his father, the king of Denmark. His grief is accentuated by his mother's unseemly and hasty marriage to his father's brother, Claudius, whom Hamlet neither likes nor trusts. Plunged into feelings of desolation, he is so despondent that he is tempted to suicide. It is only the knowledge that "self-slaughter" is a mortal sin that stays his hand.

It is when asking the key question "To be or not to be" that Hamlet struggles with the deepest matters of life and death. Is it nobler to "suffer the slings and arrows of outrageous fortune" with a patient resignation, or is it nobler "to take up arms against a sea of trouble, and by opposing end them"? Is it better to suffer injustice patiently, or is it

more noble to battle against it? Or would it not be sim-
pler simply "not to be"? To die? To commit suicide? To
escape from a living hell through the portal of death? This
is the second time that Hamlet contemplates suicide and,
for the second time, it is the fear of the consequences of
the sinful act of suicide that prevents him from taking his
own life. It is "the dread of something after death". What
if his escape from the living hell led to an everlasting hell?

From this lowest point, Hamlet then begins to move
toward an acceptance of his duty to lay down his life for the
cause of goodness, truth, and justice. In the long graveyard
scene, he once again contemplates death, but this time it is
with a spirit of Christian hopefulness. Indeed, Shakespeare
alludes to lines from a poem, "Upon the Image of Death",
by the Jesuit saint and martyr Robert Southwell, putting
the martyred saint's words onto Hamlet's lips. Soon afterward, Hamlet proclaims his faith and trust in God's providence. "There's a divinity that shapes our ends," he says to
Horatio, "rough-hew them how we will."

Later still, Hamlet alludes to the Gospel itself, asserting
that "there is a special providence in the fall of a sparrow".
With the following lines from St. Matthew's Gospel in
mind, Hamlet is saying that the very hairs of his head are
numbered by God and that, in the eyes of God, he is of
more value than many sparrows. And the verse that follows those lines in the Gospel passage is the key to understanding Hamlet's final conversion to the will of God and
acceptance of the sacrifice he must make: "Whosoever
therefore shall confess me before men, him will I confess
also before my Father which is in heaven." Hamlet is now
ready to lay down his life so that the "something rotten in
the state of Denmark" can be purged and justice and peace
restored. In the play's final scene, he lays down his life so
that his country and its people may live. It is with this "no

greater love" that Hamlet, like Christ, becomes the innocent victim who saves his people. He finally becomes the
man he is called to be by becoming like Christ. Well may
we agree with Horatio's prayer over Hamlet's dead body
that flights of angels will sing him to his rest, lines plucked
from the traditional Catholic Requiem Mass.

Worldly Wisdom and Holy Foolishness

King Lear by William Shakespeare

King Lear, like *Hamlet*, is a conversion story. Whereas Hamlet ascends from the slough of despondency to the embrace of God's will, King Lear falls from a position of great worldly power to a position of powerlessness, at which point he undergoes a radical conversion that some might see as madness.

King Lear begins with the asking of an axiomatic question: Does the king or the state have the right to demand the absolute loyalty of his or its subjects? King Lear asserts that he has such a right, demanding that his three daughters outdo each other in sycophantic praise of their love for him. The one who loves him most will have the most reward. The two wicked daughters tell him the lies he wants to hear, pretending that they love him above all else. The one virtuous daughter who genuinely loves him the most refuses to offer all her love to him, choosing instead to "love and be silent". The worldly sisters receive their worldly reward, inheriting the king's kingdom so that he can retire from the demands of government. The virtuous sister receives no worldly reward and is sent into exile. Such was the fate of Catholics in Shakespeare's own time for their refusal to practice the state religion. Cordelia, the virtuous daughter, is like St. Thomas More, who proclaims that he is the king's good servant, but God's first.

Having allowed his worldliness to make a fool of him, Lear soon realizes that the two worldly daughters have no love for him and are intent on increasing their own power by the restriction of the little power he has left. The king's Fool serves as the voice of worldly wisdom, reminding the king of his foolishness in giving away his power.

Finding himself out in the cold, quite literally, in a storm on the heath, Lear meets a different sort of fool. This is Poor Tom, who sings a Franciscan ballad while confessing his past sins and preaching the wisdom of following the commandments of God. He is dirty, almost naked, a homeless beggar who utters apparent religious gibberish. In the eyes of the worldly, such as the worldly Fool, he is nothing but a demented madman. The king, however, sees in him "the thing itself", an image of man's nothingness. Inspired by Poor Tom's holy simplicity, Lear strips himself naked in emulation of the moment of St. Francis' radical conversion. No longer desiring worldly pomp and power, Lear weds himself, like St. Francis, to Lady Poverty.

From a worldly perspective, things go from bad to worse. In the end, Lear is taken prisoner, as is the virtuous daughter, Cordelia. Yet he is far happier in his newfound humility than he ever was as a king. "Come, let's away to prison", he tells Cordelia.

> We two alone will sing like birds i' th' cage:
> When thou dost ask me blessing, I'll kneel down
> And ask of thee forgiveness: so we'll live,
> And pray, and sing, and tell old tales, and laugh
> At gilded butterflies, and hear poor rogues
> Talk of court news; and we'll talk with them too,
> Who loses and who wins, who's in, who's out;
> And takes upon's the mystery of things,
> As if we were God's spies: and we'll wear out,
> In a walled prison, packs and sects of great ones
> That ebb and flow by th' moon.

As he and Cordelia are led away to prison, he is deliri-
ously happy. "Upon such sacrifices, my Cordelia, the gods
themselves throw incense."

None of this will make sense to the worldly wise, to
the "gilded butterflies" in their fancy, fashionable clothes,
to those wealthy courtiers who spend their time talking of
court news, of who loses and who wins, who's in favor
with the powers that be and who's out of favor. Such "suc-
cessful" people are now, to the humbled and humble king,
merely "poor rogues". The worldly, wedded to wealth, do
not understand the madness of those who seek to wed Lady
Poverty. To such people, the way of the cross is the way of
foolishness. But for those who understand that sanity and
sanctity are ultimately the same thing, the holy foolishness
of St. Francis and the "madness" of King Lear are much
more true than the "wisdom" of the worldly because such
foolishness, such holiness, is nearer to heaven.

Priestly Fatherhood

The Betrothed (I Promessi Sposi)
by Alessandro Manzoni

The greatest masterpiece of Italian literature, apart from Dante's *Divine Comedy*, is probably *The Betrothed* (*I Promessi Sposi*) by Alessandro Manzoni.

First published in the early nineteenth century, *The Betrothed* is a historical novel recounting events from two centuries earlier. At the heart of the story is the agonizing relationship of Renzo and Lucia, the betrothed couple, who are swept apart by political intrigue and circumstance. It follows the hapless pair in their seemingly hopeless quest to be reunited. Against the backdrop of petty tyranny and political turmoil, and amid the mayhem of revolutionary mobs and the miasma of plague-ridden streets, the story of the lovers is interwoven with the stories of great sinners and even greater saints. Its greatest strength, however, is the menagerie of multifarious characters that Manzoni presents to the reader, often with healthy humor, a motley medley of all that is best and worst in humanity, including what is best and worst in the priesthood and the religious life.

Lucia is a worthy heroine in the tradition of great literary heroines. She shows faithful fortitude in the midst of terrible trials. She is besieged by the unwelcome advances of wicked men and beset by troubles that are not of her own making. She exhibits the powerful silence of Shakespeare's Cordelia in her resolve to refrain from the path of least resistance, retaining her virtue in the face of viciousness. She is the very icon of idealized femininity, worthy of anyone's love and warranting immense sacrifice on the part of the lover in the quest to win her hand. Renzo is utterly unworthy of her, at least at first. He is hotheaded, rash in his judgments, and rushed in his actions. His lack of prudence and temperance all too often makes matters worse. And yet he is also good and stout-hearted, lacking neither courage nor cunning. He is likable in spite of his infuriating lack of judgment. We wish him well and wish him success in being reunited with the woman of whom he is so evidently the inferior.

The novel also brings us into the presence of noble and ignoble priests, showing those who display true priestly fatherhood and those who fail to do so. In Don Abbondio and Fra Cristoforo, we are shown the worst and the best in the priesthood and the religious life. Don Abbondio is craven in his abandonment of Renzo and Lucia to the wickedness of Don Rodrigo, placing his own self-interest and material comfort over the good of his flock. In contrast, Fra Cristoforo is fearless in his pursuit of justice for the betrothed couple, striding into the very lion's den to confront Don Rodrigo.

A further example of priestly fatherhood is the depiction of the real-life historical figure of Federico Borromeo, a cousin of St. Charles Borromeo, who followed his kinsman as Cardinal Archbishop of Milan. He also followed in his kinsman's saintly footsteps as a holy servant of the Church, who was always tireless and courageous in his zeal for souls. Manzoni is dexterous in his portrayal of Borromeo's sanctity, relating it with masculine matter-of-factness without ever stooping to the saccharine level of the hagiographic.

In Don Rodrigo and the Unnamed (L'Innominato), Manzoni presents us with two fearsome tyrants, each of whom has tyrannized the weak in the wielding of power for their own self-serving purposes. In the latter, he also shows us one of the most powerful and palpable examples of spiritual conversion in all of literature, a conversion that was based on the real-life conversion of Francesco Bernardino Visconti.

And so we see how this greatest of novels shows us feminine fortitude but also masculinity in its multifaceted forms. The hotheaded young man who is too rash to be rational. The weak and cowardly priest who abandons his flock to the wolves. The courageous shepherd who stares the wolf down. The saintly bishop of the Church who serves as a priestly father to the faithful and a guide to those who have lost their way. And then there are the villains, their masculinity corrupted by machismo, who employ violence and the threat of violence to assert their self-serving dominance over others. And finally, there is the great sinner, the nameless one, who follows the footsteps of the prodigal son into the arms of the ever-forgiving Father.

Arguing but Not Quarreling

The Ball and the Cross by G. K. Chesterton

We were always arguing, G. K. Chesterton said of his relationship with his brother, but we never quarreled. This
difference between an argument and a quarrel is the difference between life and death because it is the difference
between good and evil. An argument is a bona fide seeking
of the truth. It is the use of God-given reason. A quarrel,
on the other hand, is what happens when an argument is
not conducted with charity. Once charity is lost, so is the
argument. Even if we are saying the right thing, but are
not saying it with charity, we are on the wrong side. As
St. Paul reminds us:

> If I speak in the tongues of men or of angels, but do not
> have love, I am only a resounding gong or a clanging
> cymbal. If I have the gift of prophecy and can fathom all
> mysteries and all knowledge, and if I have a faith that can
> move mountains, but do not have love, I am nothing.
> (1 Cor 13:1–2, NIV)

Chesterton's novel *The Ball and the Cross* shows us how
to argue without quarreling. It is the story of two Scots-
men, MacIan and Turnbull, an honest Catholic and an
honest atheist, who learn to see that they have more in
common with each other, as honest seekers of the truth,
than they have with almost everyone else they meet. They

care so much about the truth that they learn gradually and grudgingly to like each other and then finally to love each other. Their love of truth leads to their love of neighbor.

In contrast to this dynamic duo of truth seekers, almost everyone else in the novel couldn't care less about the truth. They ask Pilate's famous question, "Quid est veritas?" ("What is truth?" [Jn 18:38]), with a careless shrug of the shoulders, as though it were a question that is unanswerable and therefore not worth asking. MacIan and Turnbull, on the other hand, ask it with the firm commitment that it is the most important question in the world that must be asked with conviction so that the answer can be sought with conviction.

In his own life, G. K. Chesterton practiced what he preached in *The Ball and the Cross*. He argued with atheists, such as George Bernard Shaw or H. G. Wells, but he never quarreled. In consequence he remained friends with all his enemies.

In our own lives, there is much we can learn from Chesterton, as there is much we can learn from MacIan and Turnbull, the characters in his novel. In our increasingly angry and uncharitable days, we should guard ourselves against the anger and lack of charity that we see all around us. Most of us cannot succumb to anger without the risk of becoming uncharitable. There is such thing as righteous anger, as Christ shows in the Gospels when he turns over the tables in the temple, but righteous anger is only for the righteous. We should hesitate to place ourselves on such a pedestal. Perhaps the one place where we should not follow in the footsteps of Christ is in the righteous anger that turns over tables. Perhaps he is the only one who is righteous enough to have such anger. As for the rest of us, knowing that clarity is inseparable from charity, we should practice the art of arguing without quarreling.

The Necessity of Suffering

Brideshead Revisited by Evelyn Waugh

Throughout this series of reflections, we have seen how great literature wrestles with the problem of pain and seeks to penetrate to the very heart of the mystery of suffering. This is particularly true of the twentieth-century novel *Brideshead Revisited*. Its author, Evelyn Waugh, tells us in the preface to the second edition of the novel that its theme is "the operation of divine grace on a group of diverse but closely connected characters". This means that the hidden hand of Providence, the hand of God, is actually the chief protagonist of all that happens, directing the plot and writing straight with crooked lines.

If this is so, it is certainly not obviously so in the first half of the novel in which many of the key characters are making a real mess of their lives, moving further from Christ in pursuit of "happiness". If anything, we could be forgiven for thinking that God is completely absent. He is nowhere to be seen. We should remind ourselves, however, that something which is not seen is not necessarily not there. It could be hidden, or hiding itself, or it could be under our very noses, but we are too blind or too distracted to see it.

The clue to understanding God's apparent absence in the first part of the novel is given in the title of the second part: "The Twitch Upon the Thread". This is taken from a Father Brown story by Chesterton in which it is said that sinners can stray to the ends of the earth but can be brought back with a twitch upon the thread. The thread is the lifeline of grace, and the twitch upon the thread is the moment of suffering that prevents us from going where we want to go.

A more violent metaphor for suffering that Waugh employs in the novel is that of an avalanche. Two of the characters make for themselves a private space, away from the world and its worries and responsibilities, a place in which they can live in sin, only to find that their best-laid schemes come crashing down around them, crushing their hopes for "happiness". The irony is, however, that is only after they have lost everything that they thought would make them happy that they find the deep joy and peace that transcends transient pleasures. This is the love of God and his known presence in our lives, as opposed to his perceived absence.

Our hearts are restless, says St. Augustine, until they rest in God. Such rest, such peace, cannot be found in the pursuit of comfort or transient pleasures. It can only be found in the self-sacrificial love that accepts suffering as the path to peace. It is a mistake to see health, healing, and suffering as distinct or even opposing things. Suffering can be the very cause of the healing that leads to the true health that is called holiness. Indeed, health, healing, and happiness are triune. They are inseparable. Their harmonious unity is holiness itself.

"God's eternal laws are kind and break the heart of stone", says Oscar Wilde. "For how else but through a broken heart may Lord Christ enter in."[1]

God allows us to suffer because it is good for us. We might not like the medicine, it might taste bitter, but it is

---

[1] "The Ballad of Reading Gaol".

still good for us. We might not like to take up our cross, but it is good for us. The cross that we bear might cross our desires. It might make us cross. It presents us with a choice. Suffering is a crossroads in which we are invited to take the path of healing. In short and in sum, and to add one more pun, what makes us cross should make us cross ourselves!

Possessed by Our Possessions

The Hobbit by J. R. R. Tolkien

Possessions can be dangerous. If we are too attached to them, they can cause us great harm. In fact, if we are too possessive of them, we can become possessed by them. We can be possessed by our possessions. This is one of the central messages of *The Hobbit*.

In J. R. R. Tolkien's popular story, those who are possessed by their possessiveness of their possessions are said to be suffering from the dragon sickness. Smaug, the dragon, squats on his heap of treasure under the Lonely Mountain. He has no use for it, but he guards it jealously. Indeed, he guards it so jealously that he is imprisoned by it. He daren't leave his hoard for fear that someone might steal something.

The problem is that the dragon sickness doesn't only affect dragons. Anyone can suffer from it. Bilbo Baggins, the hobbit who is the hero of the story, suffers from it. At the beginning of the story, he is unwilling to go on the adventure that Gandalf prescribes for him because he is unwilling to leave his comfortable hobbit hole with all his comforting possessions. Psychologically, he is trapped in his own home. This is the very reason that Gandalf wants him to leave it. He needs to escape from its clutches. Gandalf tells Bilbo that the adventure will be good for him. It is needed as a means of healing him from the possessiveness that is possessing him.

As for the unlikely comparison and parallel between Smaug the dragon and Bilbo the hobbit, it is surely no coincidence that one squats on his possessions under a mountain while the other lives in a hobbit hole called Underhill. Since they are both suffering from the same malady, the only real difference between them is one of scale (pun intended!).

Others also suffer from the dragon sickness in *The Hobbit*, most notably Thorin Oakenshield, who is possessed by his possessiveness of the Arkenstone. It is not until he is about to die that Thorin, recognizing his affliction, offers words of hard-won wisdom to Bilbo: "If more of us val ued food and cheer and song above hoarded gold, it would be a merrier world."

The purpose of Bilbo's journey, unknown to the reluctant hobbit upon his departure but no doubt part of Gandalf's purpose in inviting him to join the dwarves, was not material wealth but spiritual health. The journey could be seen, therefore, as a pilgrimage. This is made clear by Gandalf as he accompanies Bilbo home to the Shire after the adventure. "My dear Bilbo!" the wizard exclaims. "Something is the matter with you! You are not the hobbit that you were." The wizard in his wisdom perceives that the hobbit has grown. He had grown in moral stature; he had grown in wisdom; he had grown in virtue. In short, he had grown up.

He had also gained a priceless detachment. He was no longer possessed by his possessions. He is healed of the dragon sickness.

At its deepest level, *The Hobbit* is nothing less than a profound meditation on the truth that Christ enunciates in St. Matthew's Gospel that where our treasure is, there our heart will be also.

Finding Christ in Narnia

Chronicles of Narnia by C. S. Lewis

What is it about fantasy fiction that makes it so enduringly popular?

According to Tolkien, fairy tales assist in the "recovery" of the human spirit, the "re-gaining ... of a clear view", which enables us to see things "as we are ... meant to see them."[1] Fairy stories allow us to judge the way things *are* from the perspective of the way things *ought* to be. The "should" judges the "is". This is the way things ought to be. We do not condone selfishness merely because it is normal, and nor should we. A healthy perspective always judges selfishness, and most especially our own selfishness, from the perspective of selflessness. In the language of religion, we always judge sin from the perspective of virtue, that which is wrong from the perspective of that which is right.

Fairy stories serve as a moral mirror. They can show us ourselves and the way we ought to be in the light of a Christian understanding of reality. It is in this light that we need to read and see the truths that emerge in C. S. Lewis' Chronicles of Narnia series, which are awash with Christian symbolism and deep theological perception.

The Magician's Nephew is most memorable for its analogous retelling of the Creation story from the Book of Genesis. As Aslan, the figure of Christ in all seven books,

[1] J. R. R. Tolkien, *Leaf By Niggle* (London: HarperCollins, 2001), pp. 57–58.

sings the creatures of Narnia into being, we see the role of God not merely in his divine attributes of omnipotence, omnipresence, and omniscience but in his role as the great artist, the composer of the great symphony of Creation, the source and wellspring of all beauty. There is also deep mystical significance in the words of Creation that Aslan utters: "Narnia, Narnia, Narnia, awake. Love. Think. Speak." The juxtaposition of "love", "think", and "speak" resonates with Trinitarian significance and is suggestive of the great philosophical transcendentals: the good (to love), the true (to think or reason), and the beautiful (to speak or communicate the fruits of goodness and truth through creation and creativity).

If *The Magician's Nephew* is a retelling of the Creation story in the Book of Genesis, *The Lion, the Witch and the Wardrobe* is a retelling of the Passion of Christ.

Aslan offers himself to be sacrificed in the place of Edmund, who had betrayed his family and friends to the White Witch. The Witch reminds Aslan about the "Deep Magic from the Dawn of Time": "You know that every traitor belongs to me as my lawful prey and that for every treachery I have a right to a kill." Here the Witch reveals herself as a Satan figure, the primeval traitor to whom all treachery owes its ultimate allegiance. "And so," she continues, "that human creature is mine. His life is forfeit to me. His blood is my property." Knowing that the Deep Magic cannot be denied and that justice must be done, Aslan offers himself to be sacrificed in the place of the sinner, Edmund.

In the chapter entitled "The Triumph of the Witch", we see the enactment of Aslan's passion. He has his Agony in the Garden: he is scourged, beaten, kicked, ridiculed, taunted. Finally, he is bound and dragged to the Stone Table, on which he is killed. Following his resurrection, Aslan explains "that though the Witch knew the Deep Magic, there is a magic deeper still which she did not know."

Her knowledge goes back only to the dawn of time. But if she could have looked a little further back, into the stillness and the darkness before time dawned, she would have read there a different incantation. She would have known that when a willing victim who has committed no treachery was killed in a traitor's stead, the Table would crack and death itself would start working backward.

Aslan, the sinless victim, saves the life of Edmund and, with him, the life of every other "traitor" (sinner). The death and resurrection of Aslan has redeemed the world!

Delightful stories such as those which C. S. Lewis sets in the land of Narnia remind us that we cannot enter the kingdom of heaven unless we become like little children (Mt 18:3). Since this is so, we should not think ourselves too grown up to walk with eyes of wonder through the wardrobe of the imagination into the kingdom of Narnia. If we are willing to do so, we will discover the place that every heart desires where we can live happily ever after.

Part Three

The Wisdom of G. K. Chesterton:
Twelve Reflections on the Thought
of the Great English Catholic Writer

Facts or Truth?

G. K. Chesterton was a master of paradox. It is, therefore, necessary to understand the nature of paradox if we are to understand the wisdom of Chesterton, or indeed reality itself, which is awash with paradox.

A paradox is an apparent contradiction that points to a deeper truth. One such Chestertonian paradox concerns the relationship between facts and truth. "Not facts first," Chesterton quipped, "truth first."[1] At first sight, this appears to be nothing but self-contradictory nonsense. Aren't facts true and isn't the truth a fact?

Before we dismiss Chesterton's words, we should consider the words of Christ. "The last shall be first," Christ tells us, "and the first last" (Mt 20:16, KJV). Isn't this self-contradictory nonsense? Surely, the first is not last, by definition, and the last is not first. We hesitate to accuse Our Lord of uttering nonsense, so we look for the deeper meaning in his words. We come to understand that the paradox is connected to the mystery of love. There is no greater love than to lay down our life for another. To love is to put ourselves last and the other first. If we love in this way, we will inherit the kingdom of heaven; if we refuse to love in this way, putting ourselves first, we will be

[1] Unpublished notebook, c. 1910; sourced at the G. K. Chesterton Study Centre, Bedford, England, by Joseph Pearce during research for his biography of Chesterton: *Wisdom and Innocence: A Life of G. K. Chesterton* (San Francisco: Ignatius Press, 1996) and quoted on page 83 in that book.

excluding ourselves from the kingdom of heaven. Those who put themselves last will indeed be first!

Having seen that the art of paradox is sanctified by Christ himself, we can now take a fresh look at Chesterton's paradox. In distinguishing between facts and truth, Chesterton is asking us to see beyond their apparent similarities to the difference that might exist between one and the other. Chesterton is using "fact" as something that is purely and strictly physical, whereas truth is something metaphysical. A fact is measurable scientifically. It can be quantified, weighed, or counted.

The trees that we can see are facts. We can count them. We can calculate their height. If we chop them down, we can weigh them. If we cut them into tiny pieces, we can see them under a microscope. Their molecular structure can be seen and measured. But is the tree also a good thing? Is it beautiful? Does its truth reflect the truth of God? Goodness, truth, and beauty cannot be measured physically. They are beyond the reach of physics. They transcend physics. This is why the good, the true, and the beautiful are known as the transcendentals. If facts are merely physical, trees are not merely facts. They are something else, something more.

If we can see only the physical aspects of the tree, we are blind to its goodness, truth, and beauty. We are not seeing it in its fullness, in its truth. We need to see the tree as more than a fact. We need to see it as a creature, as something created. We are meant to see it as something that exists as truth in the mind of God before it is made into the fact that we can see as a tree. "The world is charged with the grandeur of God", writes the Jesuit poet Gerard Manley Hopkins (as previously discussed). If we do not see God's grandeur in the tree, we are not really seeing it at all.

This was expressed with great beauty by another poet, Joyce Kilmer, in his poem called "Trees":

> I think that I shall never see
> A poem lovely as a tree.
>   A tree whose hungry mouth is prest
> Against the earth's sweet flowing breast;
>   A tree that looks at God all day,
> And lifts her leafy arms to pray;
>   A tree that may in summer wear
> A nest of robins in her hair;
>   Upon whose bosom snow has lain;
> Who intimately lives with rain.
>   Poems are made by fools like me,
> But only God can make a tree.

Once we learn to see the facts with the wisdom and wonder of the great poets and philosophers, we will know the truth of Chesterton's paradox. Not facts first, truth first!

Putting Happiness to the Test

What is happiness? Is it something merely fleeting? Is it beyond our reach except for brief moments of pleasure? Is pleasure happiness? What if the pursuit of pleasure wrecks our lives and the lives of others? If the pursuit of pleasure makes us miserable, can it be the same as happiness? And if happiness is not the same as pleasure, what is it? How do we know what it is? And if we don't know what it is, can we ever be happy?

G.K. Chesterton knew what happiness is, and he knew how to put it to the test. "The test of all happiness is gratitude", he wrote. He continues:

> Children are grateful when Santa Claus puts in their stockings gifts of toys or sweets. Could I not be grateful to Santa Claus when he put in my stockings the gift of two miraculous legs? We thank people for birthday presents of cigars and slippers. Can I thank no one for the birthday present of birth?[1]

The test of all happiness is gratitude because the one who lacks gratitude takes things for granted; and if we take a thing for granted, we are not able to enjoy it as a gift. Our familiarity with it breeds contempt. On the other hand, seeing it afresh as something unfamiliar allows us to be astonished anew. It restores the gift of surprise. It brings happiness.

[1] G.K. Chesterton, *Orthodoxy* (San Francisco: Ignatius Press, 1995), p. 60.

This is the reason that Chesterton is always encouraging us to stand on our heads. If we stand on our heads, we are able to see things from a new and a fresh angle. We look up and see that we have two miraculous legs. Sometimes, if we have the courage and the humility to stand on our heads, we realize that everything is suddenly the right way up and that we had always seen everything in the wrong way. We realize that we had always been standing on our heads thinking we were standing upright; now, at last, we are actually standing the right way up and can see things clearly. This process of topsy-turvydom is known as conversion. It is to cease to see the mere facts with the familiarity that breeds contempt and to see the truth with the gratitude that leads to true contentment.

"Thanks are the highest form of thought," wrote Chesterton, "and gratitude is happiness doubled by wonder."[2] In connecting gratitude and happiness to a sense of wonder, Chesterton is echoing the wisdom of the greatest of Christian philosophers, St. Thomas Aquinas, who taught that gratitude was the fruit of humility and that it was gratitude that opened the eyes in wonder. It is only when our eyes are opened in wonder, wrote Aquinas, that we are moved to the contemplation that opens the mind into the fullness of the presence of God. And here we see how and why the test of all happiness is gratitude. Without gratitude we cannot reach the fullness of the presence of God, which is the consummation and fulfillment of happiness itself. Indeed, happiness is the presence of God!

[2] G. K. Chesterton, *A Short History of England* (London: Chatto and Windus, 1929), p. 59.

"Art Is the Signature of Man"[*]

Is there a connection between the modern man in his man cave and the caveman in his prehistoric cave? Do we have much in common with our Stone Age ancestors, or does an abyss separate us? Can we understand him, and could he understand us?

Chesterton asked these questions in the first chapter of his book *The Everlasting Man*, which is entitled "The Man in the Cave":

> Today all our novels and newspapers will be found swarm-ing with numberless allusions to a popular character called a Cave Man.... His psychology is seriously taken into account in psychological fiction and psychological medi-cine. So far as I can understand, his chief occupation in life was knocking his wife about. (p. 27)

Having discussed this popular myth about the caveman, Chesterton then suggested that we do something really radical that none of those theorizing about our neolithic ancestors had thought of doing. He considered we look at the physical evidence. If we want to know about the caveman, why don't we look in the cave? If we do so, do we find piles of female skulls all neatly cracked like eggs?

* G.K. Chesterton, *The Everlasting Man* (San Francisco: Ignatius Press, 1993), p. 34. All subsequent quotations in this chapter are from this source.

Of course not. If we go into the cave, we see art on the walls. The drawings and paintings of animals "were drawn or painted not only by a man but by an artist" (p. 29).

Chesterton, who was trained as an artist before he became a writer, admired this art which "showed the love of the long sweeping or the long wavering line which any man who has ever drawn or tried to draw will recognize". He admired "the experimental and adventurous spirit of the artist, the spirit that does not avoid but attempts difficult things; as when the draughtsman had represented the action of the stag when he swings his head clean round and noses towards his tail", adding that "there are many modern animal-painters who would set themselves something of a task in rendering it truly" (p. 30).

"Art is the signature of man" (p. 34), Chesterton wrote, indicating that no abyss in terms of our shared humanity separates the man in the man cave from the man in the cave. The abyss is between man, as a creator made in the image of the Creator, and the other creatures who create nothing. There is no canine culture, no civilization of chimpanzees, no planet of the apes. Only people make music, write poetry, build cathedrals, or paint pictures. "In other words," Chesterton concludes, "every sane sort of history must begin with man as man, a thing standing absolute and alone.... This creature was truly different from all other creatures; because he was a creator as well as a creature" (p. 35).

Art is truly the signature of man. It is art that unites the caveman to the modern man. The paintings on the walls of the cave indicate the kinship of all humanity across the abyss of the ages in our shared love of beauty and our shared desire to depict that beauty through the God-given creative talents bestowed on us. In similar fashion, the earliest Christian art is also to be found on the walls of a cave, or more specifically on the walls of the catacombs.

Chesterton began the second part of *The Everlasting Man* with a chapter entitled "The God in the Cave" (p. 169). Alluding to the stable in Bethlehem, Chesterton wrote that "the second half of human history, which was like a new creation of the world, also begins in a cave.... God also was a Cave-Man, and had also traced strange shapes of creatures, curiously coloured, upon the wall of the world; but the pictures that he made had come to life" (p. 169). There is, as Chesterton implies, a delightful and divine symmetry in the history of the world that God has made and the history of the creativity with which he has made it. Human art begins in a cave. The Incarnation also begins in a cave, in the womb of the Blessed Virgin at the Annunciation, that other "cave" that Gerard Manley Hopkins described as the "warm-laid grave of a womb-life grey",[1] and is shown forth at the birth of Christ in the cave of Bethlehem. And then, a couple of centuries later, Christian art also begins in a cave. There is, therefore, a connection, set in stone, between the man in the cave and the God in the cave. That connection is the divine signature known as art.

[1] "The Wreck of the Deutschland".

"Worth Doing Badly"

Many of us were taught as children that "a thing worth doing is worth doing well". Believing this to be good and sound advice, many of us have taught our own children the very same words of apparently incontrovertible wisdom. It might come as a shock, therefore, to learn that Chesterton wrote that "a thing worth doing is worth doing badly".[1] Surely not!

We might be sorely tempted to roll our eyes at Chesterton's controversial contravening of the incontrovertible, dismissing his words as mere stupidity. Since we know, however, that Chesterton is not usually merely stupid, we should pause to ponder whether his apparent nonsense might make some sort of sense. We should consider whether he is once more playing with paradox, recalling that a paradox is an apparent contradiction pointing to a deeper truth.

Once we revisit Chesterton's words in the light of the better-known maxim that it apparently contradicts, we can see that the apparent contradiction points to a deeper understanding of those things that are worth doing well. It is not that a thing is worth doing badly *instead* of doing it well; it is that a thing is worth doing badly *because* it is worth doing well. Indeed, and this is Chesterton's point, a thing can't be done well unless it is first done badly.

---

[1] G. K. Chesterton, *What's Wrong with the World* (London: Cassell and Company, 1910), p. 254.

A few examples will illustrate Chesterton's point.

When Tom Brady first picked up a football to throw it to his father, we can be sure that he didn't throw it very far or particularly well. When Ronaldo, as a toddler, first kicked a soccer ball, which was almost as big as he was, it is likely that he didn't kick it very far. Perhaps he fell over in the very attempt to kick it, eliciting joyful laughter from his parents. Tom Brady and Ronaldo began doing things badly as a necessary prerequisite to being able to do them well. But, and this is also Chesterton's point, those who are not as gifted as Tom Brady or Ronaldo should continue to play badly because playing is good. It's better to do a good thing badly than not to do it at all, even if we will never do it particularly well.

And what is true of relatively unimportant things, such as sports, is equally true of much more important things, such as the practice of the faith. None of us were born as saints, but all of us were born to be saints. Getting to heaven is the only ultimate purpose in life. In consequence, it should be our ultimate goal, above all other lesser goals. If we find that we are not very good at becoming a saint, we should not give up the effort but should persevere, however miserably and badly we might be doing it. If we give up doing it badly, we will not be doing it at all, which is a recipe for disaster. If we persevere in doing things badly, we will do them less badly, which means that we will be doing them better. We will be making progress toward the goal, however falteringly and however often we fall or fail. There is nothing worth doing badly as much as the quest for holiness because there is nothing worth doing better. That's the paradox and that's Chesterton's point.

Believing in Anything

"When people stop believing in God, they don't believe in nothing; they believe in anything." These words are often ascribed to Chesterton, though there's no record of his ever having said them. They are, however, the sort of thing he would have said, and they are certainly Chestertonian in spirit.

When people stop believing in God, they believe in all sorts of weird and wacky things. The godless ideas of the Enlightenment led to the unleashing of the French Revolution and the enthroning of the goddess of Reason in place of the Blessed Virgin in Notre Dame Cathedral. What followed was the rule of unreason, the rule of the mob, which became known as the Reign of Terror. The godless ideas of Marx led to communist revolutions around the world with the consequent massacre of tens of millions of civilians in the name of class warfare and social "progress". The godless ideas of Nietzsche led to the rise of the Nazis and their putting of Nietzsche's idolization of power into horrific practice. In these three examples of cultures that turned their back on belief in God, we see how godlessness led to the guillotine, the gulag, and the gas chamber. More recently, a melding of the ideas of Marxist "progress" and Nietzschean "self-empowerment" has led to the killing of babies on a scale that supersedes any barbarism in history. Yes indeed. When people stop believing in God, they do believe in anything. And when people believe in anything, anything goes. And if anything goes, all hell breaks loose.

Chesterton showed how belief in God was more rational than belief in "nothing" or "anything" in his replies to Holbrook Jackson, a disciple of Nietzsche and a philosophical relativist. We will finish this reflection on the consequences of godlessness by letting Jackson and Chesterton speak for themselves:

JACKSON: Be contented, when you have got all you want.

CHESTERTON: Till then, be happy.

JACKSON: Don't think—do.

CHESTERTON: Do think! Do!

JACKSON: A lie is that which you do not believe.

CHESTERTON: This is a lie: so perhaps you don't believe it.

JACKSON: As soon as an idea is accepted it is time to reject it.

CHESTERTON: No: it is time to build another idea on it. You are always rejecting: and you build nothing.

JACKSON: Truth and falsehood in the abstract do not exist.

CHESTERTON: Then nothing else does.

JACKSON: Truth is one's own conception of things.

CHESTERTON: The Big Blunder. All thought is an attempt to discover if one's own conception is true or not.

JACKSON: No two men have exactly the same religion: a church, like society, is a compromise.

CHESTERTON: The same religion has the two men. The sun shines on the Evil and the Good. But the sun does not compromise.

JACKSON: Only the rich preach content to the poor.

CHESTERTON: When they are not preaching Socialism.

JACKSON: In a beautiful city an art gallery would be superfluous. In an ugly one it is a narcotic.

CHESTERTON: In a real one it is an art gallery.

JACKSON: Negations without affirmations are worthless.

CHESTERTON: And impossible.

JACKSON: Theology and religion are not the same thing. When the churches are controlled by the theologians religious people stay away.

CHESTERTON: Theology is simply that part of religion that requires brains.

JACKSON: Desire to please God is never disinterested.

CHESTERTON: Well, I should hope not!

JACKSON: We are more inclined to regret our virtues than our vices; but only the very honest will admit this.

CHESTERTON: I don't regret any virtues except those I have lost.

JACKSON: Every custom was once an eccentricity; every idea was once an absurdity.

CHESTERTON: No, no, no. Some ideas were always absurdities. This is one of them.

JACKSON: No opinion matters finally: except your own.

CHESTERTON: Said the man who thought he was a rabbit.[1]

[1] *Chesterton Review* 14, no. 4 (November 1988): 542–49.

The Coming Peril

What is the coming peril? Is it Marxism? Is it global warming? Many years ago, in 1927 to be precise, Chesterton gave a talk on the topic of "Culture and the Coming Peril". It was one of the best talks he ever gave and one of the most prophetic. He began by addressing the expectation of many in his audience that the "coming peril" was communism, the Bolshevik Revolution having happened only ten years earlier. Bolshevism was not a "coming peril", Chesterton quipped, because the best way of destroying a utopia was to try it. These words were themselves prophetic, in the sense that Chesterton perceived that Marxism, once put into practice, would be seen to be unsustainable.

Having dismissed Bolshevism as being unworkable, Chesterton spelled out what was the real "coming peril" threatening culture: "The danger of standardization by a low standard seems to me to be the chief danger confronting us on the artistic and cultural side and generally on the intellectual side at the moment."[1]

These portentous words ring all too true almost a century after Chesterton uttered them. The practical effects of the standardization by a low standard in modern education has resulted in declining standards of literacy and numeracy, and a woeful ignorance of history, literature, and the arts.

[1] G. K. Chesterton, *Culture and the Coming Peril* (London: University of London Press, 1927), pp. 18–19.

Whatever happened to the civilized culture that produced Shakespeare, Jane Austen, and Charles Dickens? Well, to begin with, the ongoing standardization by a low standard has meant that these great writers are not on the curriculum. Considered too challenging or, worse, "irrelevant" or "unwoke", they are ignored, glossed over, or condemned outright. They are banned and banished from the classroom. Forgetting the golden rule that we write as well as we read, the architects of modern education have abandoned the great books that offer inspiration and nurture aspiration in favor of an education for dummies that wallows on the ground zero of the banal. Fearing that any should be left behind, most are left behind. Fearing failure, most are predestined to fail.

A century after Chesterton's prophecy, the coming peril is no longer merely coming. It has come. It is here. It is upon us.

And yet there are signs of change. Families are taking matters into their own hands. They are taking the fight to the public school system, becoming active on school boards to demand an education in virtue and not in vacuity and viciousness, or they are taking their children out of the public school system all together. There has been a dramatic rise in the numbers who are homeschooling or who are sending their children to the new classical academies that are opening around the country. These healthy developments would have pleased Chesterton, who was a champion of classical education and a critic of the dumbed-down education that was in the ascendant even in his day. "The one thing that is never taught by any chance in the atmosphere of public schools", he wrote, "is ... that there is a whole truth of things, and that in knowing it and speaking it we are happy." Such words would be greeted with calculated coldness by the architects of modern education, who would no doubt respond with chilling indifference that there is no whole truth of things and therefore no meaningful happiness to be derived from it. It is no wonder that Chesterton observed that "the purpose of Compulsory Education is to deprive the common people of their common sense."[2]

Thankfully, many common people have enough common sense to fight this dumbing down of culture to a prescribed level of mediocrity. There are signs that the tide is turning. As Chesterton wrote of King Alfred the Great's defense of Christian civilization against the onslaught of Viking barbarians: "The high tide", King Alfred cried. "The high tide and the turn!"[3]

[2] G. K. Chesterton, *All Things Considered* (New York: John Lane Company, 1910), p. 153.

[3] G. K. Chesterton, *The Ballad of the White Horse* (London: Methuen, 1911), p. 147.

"The Democracy of the Dead"

There are two ways of loving our neighbors. We can love all our neighbors, which includes our enemies, or we can love only those neighbors whom we like. The first way of loving our neighbors is the way prescribed and commanded by Christ. The second way is the way of the world, the way that is not *prescribed* by Christ but is *proscribed* by him: "For if you love them that love you, what reward shall you have? do not even the publicans this? And if you salute your brethren only, what do you more? do not also the heathens this?" (Mt 5:46–47, Douay-Rheims).

Chesterton reminds us that loving our neighbors means loving all our neighbours, both the living and the dead, not merely those who happen to be alive at the same time as we. "The brotherhood of man is even nobler when it bridges the abyss of ages than when it bridges only the chasm of class."[1] We should see men of all ages as our brothers. We should see Shakespeare and Dickens as our neighbors. This should not be difficult, because they speak to us across the abyss of ages in their works. And it is through their works that we can see their neighbors through their eyes, enabling us to love them as they did.

In contrast, the modern world has a contempt for the past, which is animated by a quasi-racist assumption that the people of the past were somehow inferior to those in

---

[1] G.K. Chesterton, *The Everlasting Man* (San Francisco: Ignatius Press, 1993), p. 32.

the "enlightened" or "woke" present. Since society is always "progressing", the people of the past must be primitives who should be ignored at best or despised at worst. "It is always easy to be a modernist," wrote Chesterton, "as it is easy to be a snob."[2] This supercilious arrogance toward past generations is what C. S. Lewis called "chronological snobbery".[3] It is turning our noses up at the peasants and primitives of the past. It is considering ourselves better than they are. It is to consider ourselves part of a master race that has the right to treat the inferior people of the past with dismissive contempt, banning their books from schools and banishing their ideas from the public square.

The greatest defense against this arrogance and ignorance is the power of tradition. It is the reverence for tradition that invites our neighbors from the past to join the conversation. On the subject of tradition, as on so much else, Chesterton's words of wisdom need to be heard and heeded:

> Tradition may be defined as the extension of the franchise. Tradition means giving votes to the most obscure of all classes, our ancestors. It is the democracy of the dead. Tradition refuses to submit to the small and corrupt oligarchy of those who merely happen to be walking about. All democrats object to men being disqualified by the accident of birth; tradition objects to their being disqualified by the accident of death.... I, at any rate, cannot separate the two ideas of democracy and tradition; it seems evident to me that they are the same idea. We will have the dead at our councils. The ancient Greeks voted by stones; these shall vote by tombstones. It is all quite regular and official, for most tombstones, like most ballot papers, are marked with a cross.[4]

[2] G. K. Chesterton, *Orthodoxy* (San Francisco: Ignatius Press, 1995), p. 107.

[3] C. S. Lewis, *Surprised by Joy* (London: Fount Paperbacks [HarperCollins], 1977), p. 161.

[4] Chesterton, *Orthodoxy*, p. 53.

The Beauty of the Church Militant

God is goodness, truth, and beauty as Christ is the way, the truth, and the life. The way of goodness is love; the truth to be found through reason is ultimately Truth himself; and the life of beauty is Life himself.

And here's a paradox of Chestertonian proportions: Beauty is always alive even when it is dead. It is to be found in the life of the beholder and in the life of the beauty of the thing beheld, even if the thing beheld is not alive in the merely biological sense. This should not surprise us. God is not alive in the merely biological sense; he was alive before he created anything merely biological or anything with the sense that could sense the biological. Angels are not alive in the biological sense, nor are paintings of landscapes or portraits of people. But all these things have the life of beauty.

Even stones can come alive. Think of the sun setting behind the Rocky Mountains, or think of Michelangelo's statue of the Mother of God cradling her dead Son, or think of the great Gothic cathedrals. These things are alive with beauty even if we are not alive enough to see it. Beauty is not in the eye of the beholder but in the thing beheld. We have to be as alive as the beauty of the thing beheld to see the life of beauty in it. If we are physically blind, we will not be able to see it, which will not be our fault, but if we are metaphysically blinded by sin and cynicism, we will have killed the life of our own eyes to the beauty they were made alive to see. "Give me miraculous eyes to

see my eyes," Chesterton exclaimed, "those rolling mirrors
made alive in me, terrible crystals more incredible than all
the things they see."[1]

It is with those eyes, made alive with gratitude and
humility, that Chesterton had a vision of the living beauty
of Gothic architecture. The vision was inspired initially by
an optical illusion. He was admiring the majestic towers of
Lincoln Cathedral looming over the housetops when, suddenly, the towers began to move. "All of a sudden the vans
I had mistaken for cottages began to move away to the left.
In the start this gave to my eye and mind I really fancied
that the Cathedral was moving toward the right. The two
huge towers seemed to start striding across the plain like
the two legs of some giant whose body was covered with
clouds." Having had this vision, Chesterton's eyes were
opened in a deeper sense to the life of Gothic architecture,
"the soul in all those stones":[2]

> The truth about Gothic is, first, that it is alive, and second,
> that it is on the march. It is the Church Militant; it is the
> only fighting architecture. All the spires are spears at rest;
> and all its stones are stones asleep in a catapult. In that
> instant of illusion, I could hear the arches clash like swords
> as they crossed each other. The mighty and numberless
> columns seemed to go swinging by like the huge feet of
> imperial elephants. The graven foliage wreathed and blew
> like banners going into battle; the silence was deafening
> with all the mingled noises of a military march; the great
> bell shook down, as the organ shook up its thunder. The
> thirsty-throated gargoyles shouted like trumpets from all
> the roofs and pinnacles as they passed; and from the lectern

---

[1] "The Sword of Surprise".
[2] G.K. Chesterton, *In Defense of Sanity: The Best Essays of G. K. Chesterton*
(San Francisco: Ignatius Press, 2011), p. 71.

in the core of the cathedral the eagle of the awful evange-
list crashed his wings of brass.[3]

With eyes of gratitude, wide open with wonder, Chesterton had seen the life of Christ in the Church Militant,
made manifest in the beauty of Gothic architecture; and
then, with the gift of words, made alive by inspiration
from the Word himself, he has made his vision alive for us,
his readers, with the beauty of his poetic prose. May we
give thanks and praise to Christ, who is the Life of Beauty,
for giving such life to those who love him.

[3] Ibid.

Swimming Upstream

Is it wrong to be a reactionary? Is it better just to go with the flow? Both these questions were answered with succinct brilliance by Chesterton: "A dead thing can go with the stream," he wrote, "but only a living thing can go against it."[1] There we have it. Corpses don't react; they float downstream. Only living men swim upstream.

What does this mean with respect to faithful Christians living in a hostile culture? What does it mean with respect to the faith of the Church in such a culture? Should Christians risk being called reactionaries? Should the Church? Or should we just go with the flow of whatever is fashionable or whatever is consider politically or morally "correct"? We know how Chesterton would respond to such questions because we have his response to those in his own times who were saying that the Church should "get with the times". "We do not want a church that will move with the world", he famously quipped; "we want a church that will move the world."[2]

Chesterton knew that churches that move with the world become worldly. They cease to be witnesses to Christ and become followers of the latest fads and fashions. They don't last for long. They disappear beneath the

---

[1] G.K. Chesterton, *The Everlasting Man* (San Francisco: Ignatius Press, 1993), p. 256.

[2] Quoted in Maisie Ward, *Gilbert Keith Chesterton* (London: Sheed & Ward, 1944), p. 398.

successive waves of innovation, drowning in their own indifference to Christ, the Cross, and the Gospel. The most modern or modernist churches are those which have dwindling congregations. The paradoxical irony is that their pursuit of relevance has made them irrelevant. They become indistinguishable from the secular culture except for a few increasingly meaningless trappings.

Having heard what Chesterton had to say about the theological modernism that seeks to get with the times and go with the flow, we might wonder what Christ would say. We needn't wonder for long because he has already said it:

> Every one therefore that shall confess me before men, I will also confess him before my Father who is in heaven. But he that shall deny me before men, I will also deny him before my Father who is in heaven. Do not think that I came to send peace upon earth: I came not to send peace, but the sword. For I came to set a man at variance against his father, and the daughter against her mother, and the daughter in law against her mother in law. And a man's enemies shall be they of his own household. He that loveth father or mother more than me, is not worthy of me; and he that loveth son or daughter more than me, is not worthy of me. And he that taketh not up his cross, and followeth me, is not worthy of me. He that findeth his life, shall lose it: and he that shall lose his life for me, shall find it. (Mt 10:32–39, Douay-Rheims)

This is fighting talk. If we deny him before men, he will deny us before his Father. His denial of us is merely his acceptance of our denial of him. If we will not wield the sword of truth as he has done, we are denying him. If we will not confess the Gospel of Christ fearlessly, even in the face of persecution, we are denying him. What then of those who will not confess him for fear of flying in the face of fashion? If we will not take up our cross to follow him, we are denying him. If we seek to find our life in this world, we are denying ourselves of our life with him in heaven; if we lay down our worldly life in following him, refusing to deny him, we will find our heavenly reward with him in the eternal life promised to us.

The choice we each need to make is the choice of which spirit we choose to follow. We can choose the *Heilige Geist* or the Zeitgeist, the Holy Spirit or the spirit of the age. He who chooses the spirit of the age will move with the world; he who chooses the Holy Spirit will move the world. "The issue is now quite clear," Chesterton said on his deathbed. "It is between light and darkness and every one must choose his side."[3] Let us choose wisely. Let us choose the light of Christ, which is aflame with the Holy Spirit, and not the spirit of the world, which is a denial of the light.

[3] Ibid., p. 551.

Christianity Is Dead—
Long Live Christianity

The death of Queen Elizabeth II in 2022 should remind us that all earthly kingdoms come to an end, even the longest and most illustrious of reigns, such as hers was most assuredly. Yet, although the queen is dead, the monarchy lives on. This is symbolized by the official ritualized proclamation at the queen's death: "The queen is dead; long live the king!" Monarchs come and go, but the monarchy lives on.

And yet, for those who know history, even monarchies pass away. Where are the caesars, the czars, the kaisers, the French monarchs, the Stuart monarchs, or the Holy Roman Emperors? They are gone. They are buried by the sands of time. This mortality of monarchs and monarchies was the focus of Hamlet's wit with respect to Alexander the Great and Julius Caesar in the graveyard scene in Shakespeare's play:

> Alexander died, Alexander was buried, Alexander returneth to dust; the dust is earth; of earth we make loam; and why of that loam whereto he was converted might they not stop a beer-barrel? Imperious Caesar, dead and turn'd to clay, might stop a hole to keep the wind away.[1]

---

[1] William Shakespeare, *Hamlet*, ed. Joseph Pearce (San Francisco: Ignatius Press, 2008), 5.1.203–8.

Ashes to ashes, dust to dust. From dust we were made and to dust we shall return. And this is as true of great kings as of unknown peasants, which is why we don't merely say, "Long live the king", but "God save the king". The king needs to be saved as much as anyone else.

But what is true of kings is not true of the King of Kings, nor is it true of the Church he founded, which is his Mystical Body. The gates of hell will not prevail against it, as Christ promised (Mt 16:18), nor will the power of death.

"Christendom has had a series of revolutions," wrote Chesterton, "and in each one of them Christianity has died. Christianity has died many times and risen again; for it had a God who knew the way out of the grave."[2]

Many thought that Christianity had died when its founder had died upon the Cross. Christ was laid in a cave and rose again.

Many thought that Christianity had been killed in the wave of persecutions instigated by various "imperious caesars" during the days of the Roman Empire. The Early Church lay low in a cave and went underground, rising again from the catacombs.

Many thought that the rise of Islam would lead to the fall of the Church. The Holy Land fell to the infidel, but Holy Church rose from the ashes.

Many thought that the fall of Rome at the hands of barbarians would mean the fall of the Church of Rome. The barbarians were converted and Rome rose again because the Church of Rome had risen again.

Many thought that the so-called Dark Ages had eclipsed the light of Christ. The light was kept alive, burning before monastic tabernacles, which spread like wildfire, setting a

---

[2] G. K. Chesterton, *The Everlasting Man* (San Francisco: Ignatius Press, 1993), p. 250.

resurrected Christendom ablaze with the renewal of the light.

Many thought that the great rupture of Christendom by the Protestant rebellion had dealt a fatal blow to the Mystical Body of Christ. Yet the Church rose again in the Tridentine splendor of reinvigorated renewal.

Many thought that the rise of absolutist monarchs meant the end of the power of the Church. The monarchs and the monarchies passed away, and the Church rose again.

Many thought that the French Revolution signaled the end of the weakened Church. The Revolution destroyed itself in its own Reign of Terror, and the Church emerged, alive and well, from the shadow of the guillotine.

Many thought that the rise of Napoleon would be the knell of doom, the new emperor boasting of his power to destroy the Church. The emperor met his Waterloo, and the Church remained.

Many thought that the rise of communism would be the end of Christianity. Communism fell, and it was a Polish pope who helped to bring it crashing down.

Many thought that the Nazis would destroy the Church, crushing the Mystical Body under its merciless jackboot. The "thousand-year Reich" lasted thirteen years, and the Church lived to see its demise.

Many think in our own day and age that the latest fads and fashions will prove to be the end of Christianity. Fads fade and fashions go out of fashion. As for the future of Christianity, we need only echo the words of Chesterton that Christianity has died many times and risen again, for it has a God who knows the way out of the grave.

Faith and Fairy Stories

"My first and last philosophy, that which I believe in with unbroken certainty, I learnt in the nursery."[1] In these words of Chesterton, we find the unity of wisdom and innocence that is at the very heart of the words of Christ: we cannot enter his kingdom unless we become like little children (Mt 18:3). The paradox is that we can only remain wise in the midst of wickedness if we are as innocent as doves, or at least if we have the desire to be as innocent as doves. We must know what innocence is and desire it if we are to know what wickedness is and despise it. When we lose our innocence, we are in danger of losing our sense of wickedness. We are in danger of accepting evil and even embracing it. This is why, to employ the language of the fairytale, we must defeat the dragon that lurks in the depths of our hardened hearts. The dragon is there, and it cannot be ignored. If we fail in the quest to defeat the dragon, the dragon will succeed in its quest to defeat us.

Seeing things in this light, in the light of the nursery, in the light of innocence, we see that many great lessons can be learned from fairy stories.

"Fairyland is nothing but the sunny country of common sense", wrote Chesterton. "It is not earth that judges heaven, but heaven that judges the earth; so for me at least it was not earth that criticized elfland, but elfland that

[1] G. K. Chesterton, *Orthodoxy* (San Francisco: Ignatius Press, 1995), p. 54.

criticized the earth."² Essentially, Chesterton is reminding us that the supernatural supersedes the natural and that, therefore, metaphysics supersedes physics. God supersedes his creatures, and the things of God, such as love, reason, and beauty, supersede the purely material aspects of existence. Fairy stories teach us about love, reason, and beauty by showing their ultimate triumph over wickedness, foolishness, and ugliness, which are the negation of love, reason, and beauty and therefore their enemies.

Fairy stories are concerned with the battle between good and evil because life is about the battle between good and evil. Fairy stories show us that fighting for goodness, truth, and beauty will mean that we will live happily ever after. The Gospel shows us, and Christ promises us, that fighting for goodness, truth, and beauty will mean that we will live happily ever after.

It could be argued, of course, were we to stoop to playing devil's advocate, that fairy stories sugarcoat reality. It could be argued that reality is more messy, and more confused and confusing, than the simple good-versus-evil world that fairytales present. This is true up to a point. Fairy stories show us how things should be, not how they are. There is, however, nothing wrong with this. Christ shows us how things should be. We need to see perfection if we are to recognize our own imperfections and begin to strive toward perfection. Christ is the perfect human being, and the more like Christ we become, the more fully human we are becoming. Will we ever be as perfect as Christ? Of course not. But we will become more whole the more we become holy. The more we become the person we should be, the more fully human, the more fully real, we will become. Perfection, therefore, is not

² Ibid.

something that is unreal but, on the contrary, it is the ultimate reality to which the less real should strive so that it becomes more real.

This understanding of perfection allows us to defeat the devil's advocate and to slay the dragon of confusion that he has placed in our path. Ultimately, reality is indeed the simple good-versus-evil world that fairytales present. The whole purpose of life is to get to heaven, slaying the dragons of confusion along the way, so that we can live happily ever after with the celestial Prince Charming who has already defeated his archenemy, the Prince of Darkness. As Chesterton said, it is all about the battle between light and darkness, and each must choose his side.

Laughter and the Love of God

One of Chesterton's greatest friends, Hilaire Belloc, wrote that "there's nothing worth the wear of winning than laughter and the love of friends."[1] At first sight this might seem a somewhat trite thing to say or believe. Surely, there are much more important things than laughter and the love of friends. If, however, we include God as our best friend, the adage does not seem too far off the mark. The two great commandments of Christ are that we love the Lord our God and that we love our neighbor. There is nothing worth the wear of winning than the love of friends, such as God and our neighbors.

But what of laughter? Is laughter all that important? Chesterton certainly thought so, and he thought that God thought so too.

Chesterton hints at the divine levity and laughter in his delightful claim that "angels can fly because they take themselves lightly", whereas "Satan fell by the force of his own gravity."[2] Humility is good-humored because it takes itself lightly. Pride lacks humor because it lacks humility, taking itself too seriously. It lacks levitas because it is far too grave about its gravitas. It refuses to play the fool and falls into deeper foolishness in consequence. If this is true, it suggests that the cosmos is indeed a divine comedy, not

---

[1] "Dedicatory Ode".

[2] G. K. Chesterton, *Orthodoxy* (San Francisco: Ignatius Press, 1995), pp. 127–28.

only in the classical sense that it has a happy ending, but in the comical sense that it should make us laugh.

At this point we should remind ourselves that there is definitely something divine about laughter itself because it is evidently one of the divine attributes of man. These divine attributes are those aspects which separate man as the imago Dei from the rest of God's creatures. We are made in his image in a special way because we have certain attributes that belong to God and not to any of the other physical creatures he created. We can love as God loves; we can reason; we can create; we can see and admire beauty. And we can laugh. No other creatures laugh. It is as unique in us as is the ability to love, reason, create, and admire. It is a mark of the divine image in the imago Dei.

If this is so, why do we not see God's laughter? We can see his love, his reason, his creativity, and his beauty, but we can't seem to see him laugh. We are told in the Gospel that Jesus wept, but we are not told that he laughed. But can we believe that he didn't share the gift of laughter with his friends and disciples?

Chesterton addresses the problem and perhaps suggests an answer to the riddle at the conclusion of his book *Orthodoxy*:

> The tremendous figure which fills the Gospels ... concealed something.... There was something that He hid from all men when He went up a mountain to pray. There was something that He covered constantly by abrupt silence or impetuous isolation. There was some one thing that was too great for God to show us when He walked upon our earth; and I sometimes fancy that it was His mirth.[3]

[3] Ibid., 167–68.

Although God hides the smile or the chuckle on his own face, he shows it in the face of man, especially when the mask of flesh is removed and the grinning skull is revealed. T. S. Eliot suggests this when he speaks of the human skeleton and skull as "the rattle of bones, and chuckle spread from ear to ear",[4] but Chesterton says it best in his poem "The Skeleton":

> Chattering finch and water-fly
> Are not merrier than I;
> Here among the flowers I lie
> Laughing everlastingly.
> No; I may not tell the best;
> Surely, friends, I might have guessed
> Death was but the good King's jest,
> It was hid so carefully.

If death is the gateway to "happy ever after", it must also be a place of happy ever laughter. If death is indeed the good king's jest, we can be sure that God does not only win the final victory but that he also has the last laugh.

[4] "The Wasteland."

Part Four

Finding Christ and Manhood
in Middle-Earth:
Twelve Reflections on the
Catholic Presence in Middle-Earth

The Man Who Made Middle-Earth

J. R. R. Tolkien, the man who made Middle-earth, was a cradle convert, which is to say that he was not quite a cradle Catholic but nor was he quite a convert. He was received into the Church at the age of eight following his mother's conversion. From that time on, he remained a devout and pious practicing Catholic for the rest of his life.

Tragically, in 1904, Tolkien's mother died. His father had died eight years earlier. And so, at the age of twelve, Tolkien and his younger brother, Hilary, were orphaned. Prior to her death, Mabel Tolkien had befriended a Catholic priest, Father Francis Morgan of the Birmingham Oratory, which St. John Henry Newman had founded, whom she appointed to be the legal guardian of her two sons. It proved to be a wise choice.

Receiving little affection from the aunt with whom they were sent to live, Tolkien and his brother spent a great deal of time with the priests at the Oratory. Each morning they would serve Mass for Father Francis and then have breakfast in the refectory before setting off for school.

Tolkien remained ever grateful for all that Father Francis did for him and his brother. "I first learned charity and forgiveness from him",[1] he recalled many years later. He also remembered the opposition and hostility his mother had faced from anti-Catholic members of her family when

---

[1] Humphrey Carpenter, ed., *The Letters of J. R. R. Tolkien* (London: George Allen & Unwin, 1981), p. 354.

she was received into the Church and the sacrifices she
made for the faith:

> When I think of my mother's death ... worn out with
> persecution, poverty, and, largely consequent, disease, in
> the effort to hand on to us small boys the Faith ... I find it
> very hard and bitter, when my children stray away.[2]

As these words testify, Tolkien always considered his
mother to be a martyr for the faith. Nine years after her
death, he had written: "My own dear mother was a martyr indeed, and it was not to everybody that God grants
so easy a way to his great gifts as he did to Hilary and
myself, giving us a mother who killed herself with labour
and trouble to ensure us keeping the faith."[3]

As for Father Francis Morgan, Tolkien described him as
"a guardian who had been a father to me, more than most
real fathers".[4]

It was Father Francis who presided at Tolkien's marriage to Edith in March 1916, a marriage that would last till
death did them part at Edith's death in 1971. The couple
would have four children, three sons and a daughter. The
eldest son, John, would become a Jesuit priest.

A few weeks after the marriage, Tolkien left for the
killing fields of France and what he would call the "animal
horror" and "carnage of the Somme", one of the most
horrifically bloody battles in human history. This horror
and carnage was described graphically by Tolkien's biog-
rapher, Humphrey Carpenter:

---

[2] Ibid.

[3] Humphrey Carpenter, *J. R. R. Tolkien: A Biography* (London: George Allen
& Unwin, 1977), p. 39.

[4] Carpenter, *Letters*, p. 53.

Worst of all were the dead men, for corpses lay in every corner, horribly torn by shells. Those that still had faces stared with dreadful eyes. Beyond the trenches no-man's-land was littered with bloated and decaying bodies. All around was desolation. Grass and corn had vanished into a sea of mud. Trees, stripped of leaf and branch, stood as mere mutilated and blackened trunks.[5]

Something of this "animal horror" is evident in Tolkien's depiction of the ghoulish and ghastly Dead Marshes in *The Lord of the Rings*. On a more positive note, the courage and heroism of the ordinary soldier in the trenches inspired Tolkien's characterization of Samwise Gamgee, Frodo's trusted companion, who Tolkien said was "a reflexion of the English soldier, of the privates ... I knew in the 1914 war, and recognized as so far superior to myself".[6]

Husband, father, war veteran, scholar, storyteller, and lifelong practicing Catholic, J.R.R. Tolkien is someone whom every Catholic man can admire and, as the following reflections will show, he is also a man whose work every Catholic man can read for moral and spiritual inspiration.

[5] Ibid., p. 91.
[6] Carpenter, *J.R.R. Tolkien: A Biography*, p. 151.

Truth and Myth

As with any serious discussion on anything of importance, it is important from the beginning to define our terms. In the case of any discussion of myth, especially as the word is used by Tolkien, it is crucial that we insist that it is never used in the modern pejorative sense as meaning something that is untrue, something that is a lie. Tolkien never uses the word in this sense. For Tolkien, who was a professor of languages at Oxford University and who certainly knew the meaning of the words he used, "myth" means "story".

This crucial difference between the two meanings of the word was evident in a famous "long night talk" that Tolkien had with his good friend C. S. Lewis in 1931, which was before Lewis had become a Christian. They were discussing myth, and Lewis stated that myths were lies and therefore worthless, even though breathed through silver. In other words, myths are just beautiful lies that we might enjoy for their beauty, but that don't tell us the truth and are therefore without any intrinsic value.

"No," Tolkien replied, "they are not lies."[1] He then went on to explain how all myths contain splintered fragments of the one true light that comes from God. This was because man was made in the image of God, and his imagination, his *image*-ination, was one of the marks of the

---

[1] Humphrey Carpenter, *J. R. R. Tolkien: A Biography* (London: George Allen & Unwin, 1977), p. 151.

imago Dei, the image of God in man. God creates by bringing things into being ex nihilo, from nothing. Man creates by bringing things into being from other things that already exist, much as a landscape painter uses things that already exist, such as paint, an easel, canvas, his hands, his eyes, trees, hills, clouds, light, to bring his work of art into being. In this sense it can be said that God creates, whereas man subcreates.

Tolkien then explained that the Gospel was also a myth, in the sense that it was a story, but that it was the True Myth, in which story and truth are fully united in the realm of fact. It is the story in which God is himself the storyteller showing us that salvation history is his story of salvation. Whereas we tell our story with words, God, the Word himself, tells his story with real-life facts.

Within this True Myth of history, Christ also tells fictional stories that are nonetheless true stories. Thus, for instance, the prodigal son in Luke's Gospel (15:11–32) never existed in history. He is a fictional character, a figment of Our Lord's imagination, as are his father and brother, and the servants and the pigs. But the story is so true that everyone who hears or reads the story sees himself in the story. We don't say that the prodigal son is like us; we say that we are like the prodigal son. He is the archetype of which we are only types. In some sense, as a model of truth shown to us by Christ, even in a fictional narrative, he is more real or true than we are.

It is in this light that we can see how myths and stories can be conveyers of truth. Ebenezer Scrooge is like the prodigal son and is therefore like us. Sydney Carton in *A Tale of Two Cities* lays down his life for others at the end of the novel and is therefore, in some sense, a Christ figure, one who reminds us of Christ and reminds us that Christ has commanded us to do as he does.

Tolkien's line of reasoning was so convincing during this "long night talk" that C. S. Lewis became a Christian in consequence, proclaiming to a friend that Tolkien's eloquence had been a decisive factor in his conversion. Such is the power of friendship between good men. Such is the power of faith and reason. Such is the power of truth and myth.

"A Fundamentally Religious and Catholic Work"

The Lord of the Rings

Tolkien wrote that "*The Lord of the Rings* is, of course, a fundamentally religious and Catholic work."[1] This might surprise us because there's no mention of Christ or the Church or Christianity anywhere in the book's thousand and more pages. How can a work be religious and Catholic when there's no mention of organized religion or Catholicism?

This is a good question that can be answered only if we take Tolkien seriously. Such seriousness is demanded of us because the author knows more than anyone else about his own book. He speaks about it with authorial authority. If Tolkien tells us that *The Lord of the Rings* is a fundamentally religious and Catholic work, we should sit up and take notice. More than this. We should also sit down and read his work a little more closely.

The first thing we need to know is that Tolkien was not only a Catholic himself but also a scholar who knew and understood the Catholic Middle Ages. He knew that medieval literature was awash with references to the liturgical year, which helped convey deep theological significance to a fictional story. Take, for instance, Dante's *Divine Comedy*, perhaps the greatest work of literature ever

---

[1] Humphrey Carpenter, ed., *The Letters of J. R. R. Tolkien* (London: George Allen & Unwin, 1981), p. 172.

written. The story begins on Holy Thursday, and Dante descends into hell on Good Friday. He emerges from the depths of hell into the light of the sun at the foot of Mount Purgatory on Easter Sunday morning.

In similar fashion, the story of Sir Gawain and the Green Knight, which Tolkien translated into modern English, begins in the Christmas season and reaches its climax on the following Christmas. In addition, Sir Gawain sets out on his penitential quest on All Souls' Day, a day of penance when we pray for the suffering souls in purgatory, and finds himself in a desert during the penitential season of Advent. His prayers are answered on Christmas Eve, enabling him to fulfill his quest.

Tolkien uses the same method to convey theological significance in *The Lord of the Rings*. We are told that the Ring is destroyed on March 25, which is perhaps the single most important date on the Christian calendar. This is the date of the Annunciation, the date on which the Word becomes flesh; the date on which God becomes Man. Need we remind ourselves that the Annunciation is even more important than Christmas because life begins at conception, not at birth? God became Man on March 25, nor December 25.

March 25 is also considered by Christian tradition to be the historical date of the Crucifixion and is ascribed by Jewish tradition as the date of Abraham's sacrifice of his son Isaac, which is itself seen by Christian theologians as a mystical prefiguring of the Father's sacrificing of his Son on Calvary.

Let's remind ourselves that the Incarnation and the Crucifixion, taken together with the Resurrection, destroy the power of sin. Seen in this theological light, Tolkien's naming of March 25 as the date on which the power of the Ring is destroyed connects the destruction of the Ring with the destruction of sin itself. This is the hidden key that, once discovered, unlocks the deepest elements of the "fundamentally religious and Catholic" dimension of *The Lord of the Rings*.

The One Sin to Rule Them All and in the Darkness Bind Them

Once we have discovered that the Ring is destroyed on March 25, we realize the connection between the power of the Ring and the power of sin. The Ring is the One Ring to rule them all and in the darkness bind them. Original Sin is the One Sin to rule them all and in the darkness bind them. The One Ring and the One Sin are both destroyed on the same theologically crucial date. This enables us to see the Ring's power in the light, or should we say the shadow, of sin.

Placing the Ring on our finger is the act of sin. When we put the Ring on, we become invisible to the light of the good world that God has created. We have excommunicated ourselves from all such goodness. For as long as we keep the Ring on, we remain in darkness. Excommunicated. While we are in this land of shadow, we fall increasingly under the power of darkness. Sauron, the demonic dark lord, can see us and influence us much more easily when we have chosen the darkness over the light. If we keep the Ring on or keep putting it on habitually, we become addicted to its power, compromising our very freedom and our very ability to escape its satanic presence. We begin to fade. We begin to shrivel and shrink into a shrunken wreck. We become like Gollum. We gollumize ourselves. In gripping the Ring, we become gripped by it. In possessing it, we become possessed by it. In wearing the Ring, in living in sin, we are playing with the fire of hell.

There is, however, another way of handling the power of the Ring. If we choose to bear it but refuse to wear it, we grow in virtue. The Ring-bearer accepts the weight and the burden of sin without succumbing to the power of sin. He bears the weight of the Ring for his own sake, but also, and crucially, he bears it for the sake of others. In Christian terms, bearing the weight of sin through the acceptance and embrace of suffering is taking up our cross. In this sense, we can say that the one who carries the Ring is not merely a ring-bearer but a cross-bearer.

There is, however, a problem. None of us has the strength to bear the weight of the Ring, the weight of sin, the weight of the cross. We need help. We need the help of those whom we are commanded to love. We need the help of our God and the help of our neighbor. Frodo, the Ring-bearer, needs the help of the Fellowship of the Ring. He needs the help of his trusted friend, Samwise Gamgee. But he also needs the help of God. "There was more than one power at work," Gandalf tells Frodo, a power that was beyond the power of the dark lord, "beyond any design of the Ring-maker".[1]

"I can put it no plainer", says Gandalf, "than by saying that Bilbo was *meant* to find the Ring, and *not* by its maker. In which case you were *meant* to have it. And that might be an encouraging thought."[2]

We'll leave our contemplation of the power of the Ring and the power of sin on that encouraging thought. Next, we'll find further encouragement in the light that penetrates all darkness.

---

[1] J. R. R. Tolkien, *Lord of the Rings* (Boston/New York: Houghton Mifflin Company, 2004), pp. 55–56.
[2] Ibid.

"Above All Shadows Rides the Sun"

Though here at journey's end I lie
in darkness buried deep,
beyond all towers strong and high,
beyond all mountains steep,
above all shadows rides the Sun
and Stars forever dwell:
I will not say Day is done,
Nor bid the Stars farewell.[1]

These words were sung by Samwise Gamgee in one of the darkest moments in *The Lord of the Rings*. They are sung at a time when Sam believes Frodo to be dead and when he has himself come to "a dead end". All seems lost. The quest to destroy the Ring has apparently ended in futile failure. Yet the words he sings are not words of despair but of hope. Instead of surrendering to suicidal despair, he raises his heart to the heavens and knows that there is a light above all darkness and beyond the reach of any shadow of evil.

In this darkest of moments, Sam is doing what we are all called to do in such moments. He looks up.

It is no coincidence that the Greek word for man is *anthropos*, which means he who turns upward. The ability and the desire to turn upward is what makes a man. We are not merely animals constrained by instinct; we are

[1] All quotations for this chapter taken from J. R. R. Tolkien, *Lord of the Rings* (Boston/New York: Houghton Mifflin Company, 2004).

creatures made in the image of God who are called to gaze in wonder at the heavens seeking and seeing the metaphysical truth beyond the mere physical facts. This is what makes us different from the rest of the beasts of the field. The animal grazes, but man gazes!

In Middle-earth the presence of God or the prevalence of Providence is often communicated in terms of a light from above that penetrates the darkness. In *The Hobbit* the secret entrance to the Lonely Mountain is illuminated by the last light of the setting sun when a finger of sunlight descends from the heavens to point to the hidden door. It might remind us, and perhaps it should remind us, of the most famous finger in all of art, that of God himself touching the fingertip of Adam in Michelangelo's fresco on the ceiling of the Sistine Chapel.

There is a similar scene in *The Lord of the Rings* at the Cross-roads of Ithilian. Frodo and Sam come across the seated statue of an old king, gnawed with age and maimed by the violent hands of devil-worshipping orcs. The king's head has been hacked off and replaced with an ugly rough-hewn stone on which is daubed a hideously grinning face with one large red eye, the symbol of Sauron, the dark lord. The whole scene sickens Frodo and Sam. The beautiful statue, defaced with obscene graffiti and defiled by worshippers of the devil, has been destroyed by those who hate beauty as they hate goodness and truth. It seems to symbolize the triumph of evil over civilized culture. But then, the level rays of the setting sun illuminate the discarded head of the statue. "Look!" Frodo cries. "The king has got a crown again!" (p. 702).

The eyes were hollow and the carven beard was broken, but about the high stern forehead there was a coronal of silver and gold. A trailing plant with flowers like small

white stars had bound itself across the brows in reverence
for the fallen king, and in the crevices of his stony hair
yellow stonecrop gleamed. (Ibid.)

It's as though God's creation, the flowers of silver and
gold, illumined by a finger of sunlight through the trees, has
crowned the civilized culture of man. Divine art crown-
ing human art. Heartened by this divine revelation of God's
presence and blessing, Frodo finds new strength. "They
cannot conquer forever!" he exclaims (ibid.).

Like Frodo, we are meant to look to the heavens, seeking the light that transcends all darkness. This was what
Tolkien's friend Roy Campbell was doing when he wrote
his sonnet "To the Sun":

> Oh let your shining orb grow dim,
> Of Christ the mirror and the shield,
> That I may gaze through you to Him,
> See half the miracle revealed.

We are not meant to worship the sun, though we might
understand why the pagans did so, seeing it as the giver of
light and life. We are meant to worship the one who made
the sun. Above all shadows rides the sun because above all
shadows rides the Son!

Seeing Christ in Middle-Earth

The dignity of the human person and the sanctity of human life is rooted in the fact that we are all made in God's image. We are meant to love our neighbor because in some sense we are meant to see God's image in each of our neighbors. We are meant in some mystical sense to see the face of Christ in the face of a stranger. This is not very easy, especially when our neighbor behaves wickedly, acting in prideful defiance of the divine image in which he is made. In great works of literature, however, we can see characters who are Christ figures, who remind us in some way of Christ. This is especially so with *The Lord of the Rings*.

There are three characters in *The Lord of the Rings* who are in some sense Christ figures. Each of these conforms in some way to our understanding of Christ as priest, prophet, and king.

The priest is Frodo, who takes up his cross, sacrificing himself for the salvation of all the peoples of Middle-earth, even unto death. We have already seen that the One Ring represents the power of sin. The one who wears the Ring is the one who chooses to sin. If, however, we choose to be a Ring-bearer and not a Ring-wearer, we are shouldering the burden of sin without sinning. We are taking up our cross. In this sense, Frodo as the one ordained to be the Ring-bearer is the Cross-bearer. This is made clear from the fact that Frodo leaves Rivendell on December 25 and arrives at Mount Doom

(Golgotha) on March 25. Frodo's journey represents the life of Christ from his birth to his death.

The character in *The Lord of the Rings* who represents Christ in his calling as a prophet is Gandalf. This is seen in Gandalf's supernatural knowledge of what the future holds and the way he guides others in the light of such knowledge. It is no coincidence that Gandalf dies fighting the demonic Balrog, nor that he is later resurrected from the dead, after which he is no longer Gandalf the Grey but Gandalf the White, his robes so dazzlingly white that it seems as if the sun shines through him. In his death, resurrection, and transfiguration, there is no mistaking Gandalf's role as a Christ figure.

Finally, there is the character who represents Christ the King. This is Aragorn, the true king who comes in humility, not in glory, to serve his calling and save his people. The hands of the king are the hands of a healer, says the wise woman of Gondor, and Aragorn's healing power is the sign by which his kingship is recognized. It is also said that only the true king can take the Paths of the Dead and survive. Aragorn takes the Paths of the Dead and not only survives but has the power to release the dead themselves from their curse. His descent into the land of the dead and his emergence with the army of the liberated dead in his train reminds us insistently of Christ's descent into hell following his death, releasing the souls confined there so that they can follow him to the kingdom of heaven.

Tolkien is more subtle in his revelation of Christ than his good friend, C. S. Lewis, who gives us only one Christ figure in all seven books of the Chronicles of Narnia. Aslan is always and at all times the Christ figure in all the stories. Tolkien gives us three separate characters, none of whom are unequivocal Christ figures like Aslan, but each of whom shows us the presence of Christ in Middle-earth.

And there's one other way that Tolkien shows us Christ, and that's in the way-bread called lembas, which has the power to feed the will and is the only thing that Frodo and Sam have to eat during their time in the lifeless desert of Mordor. We are told that "lembas" means "life-bread" or the "bread of life", connecting the "magic" bread that feeds the hobbits with the miraculous Bread of Life with which Christ feeds all those who are in communion with him.

Seeing Ourselves in Middle-Earth

Tolkien said in his famous essay "On Fairy-Stories" that fairytales hold up a mirror to man. They show us ourselves. This being so, we shouldn't be surprised to find several Everyman figures in *The Lord of the Rings*, those characters who represent us in some way or other.

First and foremost, in a general sense, we can see that the hobbits represent us. "I am, in fact, a hobbit in all but size", Tolkien said of himself. "I like gardens, trees, and unmechanized farmlands; I smoke a pipe, and like good plain food."[1] Like hobbits, most of us are creatures of comfort who are in danger of becoming addicted to the creature comforts. This is why we need to go on adventures, however inconvenient they might be or how uncomfortable, or even how potentially dangerous. We cannot be the hobbits we're meant to be unless we are prepared to leave the sanctuary of our hobbit holes, our comfort zones, and embrace the perilous adventure of life, which is nothing less than the quest for heaven.

Another Everyman figure in *The Lord of the Rings* is Boromir, who is the official representative of humanity in the Fellowship of the Ring. The Fellowship consists of four hobbits, an elf, a dwarf, a wizard, a king, and a man. Boromir is, therefore, literarily an Everyman figure because he is literally the one man who represents all men. This is a sobering thought because Boromir is the one who

---

[1] Humphrey Carpenter, ed., *The Letters of J. R. R. Tolkien* (London: George Allen & Unwin, 1981), p. 288.

betrays the Fellowship, trying to steal the Ring from Frodo that he might use it to defend his country and people from the imminent invasion of the demonic armies of Mordor. He sees the power of the Ring as a gift with which to fight evil, but he forgets that we can't use evil means to a good end. If we do so, we don't defeat evil, we become evil.

In spite of his pride and foolishness, Boromir dies defending the hobbits, laying down his life for his friends. There is no greater love than this, as Christ tells us (Jn 15:13). In his final moments, he confesses his sins to Aragorn, following precisely the form of the sacrament of penance. He shows contrition, confesses his sin, and makes satisfaction for his sin in the ultimate act of laying down his life.

Another Everyman figure, apart from Boromir, is Faramir, Boromir's brother. Faramir says that he would not pick up the Ring if he found it lying at the side of the road. He also says that he would not snare even an orc with a falsehood. He would not tell even the smallest lie to the devil himself. Unlike his brother, he is not willing to use evil means to a good end, irrespective of the apparent smallness of the evil or the greatness of the good. If Boromir is the repentant sinner, much like us, Faramir is the saint. Boromir shows us who we are; Faramir shows us who we should be.

There is, however, one other Everyman figure whom it perilous to overlook. This is Gollum, who is so addicted to the power of sin that he desires nothing but to remain in its power. He has become what St. Paul would call a slave to sin (Rom 6:17). The frightening thing is that Gollum shows us the shriveled shrunken wreck we will become if we succumb to the power of sin. In choosing sin we are choosing to gollumize ourselves.

And so, we see how Tolkien presents Everyman figures in *The Lord of the Rings* to show us who we are, who we should be, and who we shouldn't be.

The God of Creation in Middle-Earth

We have seen how Tolkien shows us Christ in Middle-earth and how he shows us ourselves reflected in the story. But what of Middle-earth itself? Is it like our own earth?

Tolkien stated explicitly that Middle-earth isn't merely like our own earth but that it is our own earth imagined as it might have looked tens of thousands of years ago. If this is so, and since Tolkien was a believing Catholic, we should not be surprised to discover that Tolkien's account of the creation of Middle-earth harmonizes and dovetails with the account of the Creation given in the Book of Genesis.

The creation story that Tolkien gives us in *The Silmarillion* begins with the same words with which Genesis begins and, indeed, the same words with which St. John begins his Gospel: "In the beginning ..."

In the beginning there was Eru, the one God whom the elves named Ilúvatar, which means All-Father or the Father-of-All. We see, therefore, that Middle-earth is not a polytheistic cosmos with many gods; still less is it an atheistic cosmos with no God; it is a monotheistic cosmos with one God who is known as the Father.

God is presented by Tolkien as the composer of the symphony of creation, which is known as the Great Music. But God doesn't command the angelic beings who are the firstborn of his thought to listen to the Music he has composed; he commands them to play it. This is deep Christian theology. God is the Creator, and those made in his image are subcreators who are called to make by the creative law in which they're made. Angels and men are not merely creatures, like other creatures; they are also called to be creators. Their imagination is the mark of the imago Dei, the image of God in which they're made. The imagination is the *image-ination* with which we create as we are created. We compose music; we paint pictures; we write poetry; we tell stories.

Since, however, we are fallen and broken creatures who abuse our freedom, we often abuse our gifts for evil purposes. And so we see that Melkor, the mightiest of the angels, refuses to use his gifts of music to play in harmony with the Composer's will but weaves malicious, dark, and ugly themes into the Great Music. Disharmony enters the cosmos.

Melkor is cast from heaven into the void in language that echoes the description of the fall of Lucifer in the Book of Isaiah: "How art thou fallen from heaven, O Lucifer, son of the morning!" (14:12, KJV). This is how Tolkien describes the fall of Melkor:

> From splendour he fell through arrogance to contempt for all things save himself, a spirit wasteful and pitiless. Understanding he turned to subtlety in perverting to his own will all that he would use, until he became a liar without shame.[1]

Whereas Lucifer means "light-bringer" or "light-bearer", a reference to his being the brightest of the angels prior to his fall into darkness, Melkor means "mighty one" because he is the mightiest of the angels. Following his

---

[1] J. R. R. Tolkien, *The Silmarillion* (London: George Allen & Unwin, 1979), p. 34.

fall, Lucifer forfeits his name and is known simply as Satan, which means "enemy" or "adversary". Similarly, Melkor forfeits his name and is known instead as Morgoth, "the Dark Enemy of the World". It is clear, therefore, since Middle-earth is our own earth, that Melkor and Morgoth are merely the names that Tolkien gives in his stories to Satan. It is to the forces of darkness that we will now turn our attention.

Finding the Devil in Middle-Earth

We have seen in the previous reflection how Satan is known in Middle-earth as Melkor or Morgoth. He does not make a direct appearance in *The Lord of the Rings*, but he is present in the satanic presence of Sauron, the Dark Lord, who is Satan's greatest servant or slave:

> Among those of [Melkor's] servants that have names the greatest was that spirit whom the Eldar called Sauron.... In all the deeds of Melkor the Morgoth ... Sauron had a part.... He rose like a shadow of Morgoth and a ghost of his malice, and walked behind him on the same ruinous path down into the Void.[1]

Apart from the demonic presence of Sauron, other figures and characters in *The Lord of the Rings* are demonic or are servants of demonic power. The Balrog, which Gandalf confronts and fights in the Mines of Moria, is one of a legion of demons that Tolkien describes as "dreadful spirits ... scourges of fire" and "demons of terror".[2]

Saruman forfeits his title as Saruman the White after he is corrupted by the desire to harness the power of the Ring. In choosing to serve the powers of darkness, he renounces the whiteness of his robes, which denotes the purity of truth

[1] J. R. R. Tolkien, *The Silmarillion* (London: George Allen & Unwin, 1979), p. 35.
[2] Ibid., p. 31.

143

and reason, declaring himself to be Saruman of Many Colors. In doing so, he is echoing the prideful philosophy of Nietzsche, who declared that "God is dead" and that those who would be "Supermen" must go beyond good and evil. In choosing the many-colored rainbow over the goodness and purity symbolized by his white robes, Saruman declares himself to be a relativist and a servant of nothing but his own pride and the madness of its narcissistic ambition.

Another evil character is Wormtongue, whose very name denotes his satanic leanings. The word "worm", or *wyrm* in Old English, means "serpent" or "dragon". When Gandalf calls Wormtongue "a snake", Wormtongue "hisses" his reply. "Down on your belly, snake!" Gandalf commands, echoing God's condemnation of Satan, whose wormtongue had tempted Adam and Eve into sin. Ever the Catholic theologian, Tolkien's depiction of evil always resonates with biblical applicability. Such is his depiction of evil as being dark, black, or shadowed, reflecting his Augustinian understanding of evil as being a privation, as nothing but the absence of the good.

We'll end our hunt for the devil in Middle-earth with a consideration of the palantiri, the seeing stones into which it is perilous to look.

The perilous nature of the seeing stones is that the one peering into them only sees what the dominant will wants him to see. It's not necessarily that one is seeing a lie, but one is only seeing that part of the truth that the dominant will chooses to show. Denethor spends so much time peering into one of the palantir stones, watching the one-sided propaganda that Sauron is showing him, that he becomes convinced that evil must triumph and that it is futile to resist. Succumbing to the mortal sin of despair, he commits suicide, imperiling the people of Middle-earth in the process. It is intriguing, therefore, that "palantir" translates from the elvish as "television"! This is surely a deliberate joke on Tolkien's part but a joke with a serious message. Tolkien seems to be showing us in the downfall of Denethor that becoming addicted to the news, as presented by those who control the media, is dangerous to our very souls. To put the matter bluntly, if we watch too much TV, we might lose hope that the dark lords of the media can be resisted. Tolkien was dismayed by the way that the radio was used during World War Two for the propagation of propaganda, in other words for the systemic telling of lies. He must have feared, when he was writing *The Lord of the Rings*, what powers would be unleashed by the new technology of television. What he feared for the future has become reality in the present. The moral is clear enough. Pray often, find time to read good books such as *The Lord of the Rings*, but don't be tempted to look into the palantir stone that each of us now keeps in our home!

Hobbits and the Habits
We Need to Break

In a hole in the ground there lived a hobbit. Not a nasty, dirty,
wet hole. . . . It was a hobbit-hole and that means comfort.[1]

When we think of hobbits, we think of "home" and
"habit" and of the comforts of home. And this is their
weakness. They are so possessive of their possessions that
they are possessed by them. They are trapped within their
own self-constructed comfort zones. They are creatures of
comfort addicted to the creature comforts.

In Christian terms, hobbits are dedicated to the easy life
and find the prospect of taking up the cross and following
the heroic path of self-sacrifice utterly unappealing. This is
why Gandalf prompts Bilbo to go on an adventure. Gandalf knows that Bilbo can grow in wisdom and virtue only
if he leaves his comfort zone. He must abandon his material wealth so that he can gain his spiritual health.

When Bilbo arrives home, more than a year after his
departure, he is shocked to find that the contents of his
home are being auctioned and that most of his treasured
belongings have already been sold. The auction was adver-
tised as a sale of the property of "the late Bilbo Baggins
Esquire" who was "Presumed Dead".

[1] J. R. R. Tolkien, *The Hobbit* (London: Harper Collins, 1988), p. 13.

Bilbo rises from his presumed death, gatecrashing his own "funeral". Ironically, he had been "dead" before he set out on his adventure, or at least not as fully alive. His adventure had changed him. It had brought him to life, or at least to the fullness of life. It was the death of the old hobbit and the birth of the new. He had been "born again". In this sense the perception of his resurrection from the dead upon his return is a reflection of a deep spiritual reality. Bilbo had indeed been dead but is now alive.

There is, however, a price to pay beyond the mere loss of his worldly possessions. In spite of the new life that is in him, or perhaps because of it, Bilbo "had lost his reputation ... he was no longer quite respectable".[2] But the "resurrected" Bilbo cares little for worldly respectability. If he is dead in the eyes of the world, it is because he is dead to the world. He no longer seeks the things that the world has to offer, having discovered the pearl of great price that the world does not value. "He was quite content: and the sound of the kettle on his hearth was ever after more musical than it had been even in the quiet days before the Unexpected Party."[3]

Home is sweeter for the absence. Everything is made new, even the smallest things, *especially* the smallest things, such as the kettle on the hearth. The new Bilbo sees the old things with new eyes, and he sees that they are good, indeed better than he had ever imagined them to be.

In the final conversation between Gandalf and Bilbo, with which the story concludes, Gandalf reminds the hobbit that he is but a small part of a much bigger providential picture:

[2] J. R. R. Tolkien, *The Hobbit* (London: Grafton, 1991), p. 282.
[3] Ibid., pp. 282–83.

"You don't really suppose, do you, that all your adventures and escapes were managed by mere luck, just for your sole benefit? You are a very fine person, Mr Baggins, and I am very fond of you; but you are only quite a little fellow in a wide world after all!"

"Thank goodness!" said Bilbo, laughing.[4]

The final paradox, worthy of Jesus Christ, the Master of paradox as he is the Master of everything else, is that the purpose of Bilbo's pilgrimage was to enable him to grow big enough to know how small he is. The greatest gift that Bilbo receives from all his adventures is the poverty of spirit that enables him to seek those treasures of the heart to be found in wisdom and virtue. He is healed and is whole, or, as Tolkien the Catholic might say, he is whole because he is holy. Having attained the habit of virtue, the hobbit knows what is necessary to live happily ever after as befits the hero of any good fairy story.

[4] Ibid., p. 285.

Fighting the Long Defeat

"I am a Christian," Tolkien wrote, "and indeed a Roman Catholic, so that I do not expect 'history' to be anything but a 'long defeat'—though it contains ... some samples or glimpses of final victory."[1] This concept of history was taken up by Galadriel in *The Lord of the Rings* when she proclaimed that she and her husband "through ages of the world [had] fought the long defeat". Isn't this view of history a little pessimistic? Isn't this talk of a "long defeat" a little defeatist? Shouldn't we be focusing on the final victory and not worrying about endless defeat?

These are good questions, but they can be answered correctly only if we understand the defeat of which Tolkien is speaking and the final victory that he glimpses.

Tolkien knew that the final victory is not to be found in the long defeat of human history but in the place where all defeat has been defeated. "My kingdom is not of this world", Christ tells us. "If my kingdom were of this world, my servants would certainly strive that I should not be delivered to the Jews: but now my kingdom is not from hence" (Jn 18:36, Douay-Rheims).

The glorious truth is that the final victory is not thousands of years in the future but at the end of the world, which, for each of us, is the moment of our own individual deaths. Victory is not when the curtain finally falls

---

[1] Humphrey Carpenter, ed., *The Letters of J. R. R. Tolkien* (London: George Allen & Unwin, 1981), p. 255.

on the long defeat of history, at the final apocalypse, but when the curtain finally falls on us. The end of the world is the end of our lives. What follows at that very moment, which could be as soon as today, is the final victory or the final defeat. We will either exchange the long defeat for the final victory or else we will exchange the long defeat for the final defeat. There is no other future for any of us when our own particular world ends.

It is crucial, therefore, that we keep our eyes on the glimpses of victory. It's not for us to know, or even particularly to care, what battles will be fought after our own particular battle has ended. Since all of time is simultaneously present to the One who brings it into being, the future is in safe hands.

As for the past, Tolkien's great friend C.S. Lewis reminds us that the whole of history is enlightened by those who fought the long defeat by keeping their eyes on the final victory:

> If you read history you will find that the Christians who did most for the present world were just those that thought the most of the next. The Apostles themselves, who set on foot the conversion of the Roman Empire, the great men who built up the Middle Ages, the English Evangelicals who abolished the Slave Trade, all left their mark on Earth, precisely because their minds were occupied with Heaven. It is since Christians have largely ceased to think of the other world that they have become so ineffective in this. Aim at Heaven and you'll get earth "thrown in": aim at earth and you'll get neither.[2]

The lesson of history is simple enough. If we keep our eyes on heaven, we will make the world a better place;

[2] C.S. Lewis, *Mere Christianity* (San Francisco: HarperSanFrancisco, Harper edition, 2001), p. 134.

if we lose sight of heaven, we will be making the world even worse than it is already. It is, therefore, necessary to see the defeat by the light of the victory, and not the other way round. If we fight the long defeat with the things of heaven in mind, we will attain the final victory. It is this final victory that represents, for each of us, the final defeat of the prince of this world.

Tolkien and the Meaning of Life

As we finish our series of reflections on Middle-earth, we will let Tolkien have the final word.

In 1969, when Tolkien was seventy-seven years old, he received a letter from a young girl, who asked him, as part of a school project, "What is the purpose of life?"[1] His reply offers priceless insights into the deep Catholic philosophy that informed his life and work.

He began with primal principles, insisting that the very raising of the question of "purpose" suggests the presence of "mind". "Only a Mind can have purposes", he says, adding that the presence of "Mind" prompts necessary questions about the presence of God: "Is there a God, a Creator-Designer, a Mind to which our minds are akin (being derived from it) so that It is intelligible to us in part?" (pp. 399–400). The asking of such a question brings us to religion "and the moral ideas that proceed from it". The inextricable connection between "purpose" and "mind" is crucial to answering any questions relating to the purpose of life because such a connection is necessary to the very asking of the questions: "If you do not believe in a personal God the question: *What is it the purpose of life? Is unaskable and unanswerable*" (ibid.). We can't answer a question that we can't ask!

---

[1] All quotations taken from Humphrey Carpenter, ed., *The Letters of J. R. R. Tolkien* (London: George Allen & Unwin, 1981), pp. 399–400.

Having asked and answered these axiomatic questions, Tolkien proceeded to the purpose of life itself:

> The chief purpose of life, for any one of us, is to increase according to our capacity our knowledge of God by all the means we have, and to be moved by it to praise and thanks. To do as we do in the *Gloria in Excelsis*: Laudamus te, benedicamus te, adoramus to, glorificamus te, gratias agimus tibi propter magnam gloriam tuam. We praise you, we call you holy, we worship you, we proclaim your glory, we thank you for the greatness of your splendour.
>
> And in moments of exaltation we may call on all created things to join in our chorus, speaking on their behalf, as is done in Psalm 148, and in The Song of the Three Children in Daniel II. PRAISE THE LORD ... all mountains and hills, all orchards and forests, all things that creep and birds on the wing. (Ibid.)

These beautiful and glorious words of praise to God the Father are echoed in words of praise to God the Son, as made manifest in the Eucharist:

> Out of the darkness of my life, so much frustrated, I put before you the one great thing to love on earth: the Blessed Sacrament.... There you will find romance, glory, honour, fidelity, and the true way of all your loves on earth, and more than that: Death: by the divine paradox, that which ends life, and demands the surrender of all, and yet by the taste (or foretaste) of which alone can what you seek in your earthly relationships (love, faithfulness, joy) be maintained, or take on that complexion of reality, of eternal endurance, which every man's heart desires. (pp. 53–54)